The BossQueen,

Little BigBark,

and the Sentinel Pup

The BossQueen, Little BigBark, and the Sentinel Pup

by Sarah Clark Jordan

TRICYCLE PRESS
Berkeley | Toronto

Tricycle Press
a little division of Ten Speed Press
P.O. Box 7123
Berkeley, California 94707
www.tenspeed.com

Book design by Chloe Rawlins
Cover artwork and dog icons by Michael S. Wertz
Typeset in Stempel Garamond and Mrs Bathhurst

Library of Congress Cataloging-in-Publication Data
Jordan, Sarah Clark, 1955–
   The BossQueen, Little BigBark, and the Sentinel Pup / by Sarah Clark Jordan.
      p. cm.
   Summary: Young Mina must find her place in the order of things when she
and the two older dogs move with OurShe into a different house, where the
new members of their pack include OurHe, OurBoy, OurGirl, and That Cat.
   ISBN 1-58246-115-5
   1. Dogs--Juvenile fiction. [1. Dogs--Fiction. 2. Cats--Fiction. 3. Human-animal
relationships--Fiction. 4. Moving, Household--Fiction.] I. Title.
   PZ10.3.J825Bo 2004
   [Fic]--dc22
                                    2004000765

First Tricycle Press printing, 2004
Printed in the USA
   2 3 4 5 6 — 08 07 06 05

This book is dedicated to all good Dogs:

Jenny, Rody, Maxie, Betsy, Sam and his two girls,
Winter, Shelby, Cody, Bandito, Puppet, Snoopy,
Harmony, Jessie, Billy, Chinook, the Three Terriers
at Atria, Grom, Foxy, Piff, Mighty Joe, Sparky,
Shy Dog, Major, Goldie, Bear, Revay, Daphne,
Ginger, Brandy, Monty, Starbuck, Sissy, Sassy, Tip,
Cubbie (she smiles!), Blue, Pooh, Bud, Cocoa, Pearl,
Heidi, Tuxedo, Good Dog, Amazing Gracie, Saga,
Shandy, Buddy, Saint Sunny, Darby, Milo, Cotton,
Lacy, Scout, Dino, Guido, and Haru;

and especially to my sister, Flo, and her Dogs,
Chris, Layla, and Mina;

and to your Dog.

TheGirls

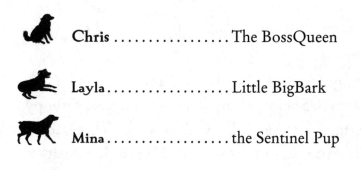

Chris . . . . The BossQueen

Layla . . . . Little BigBark

Mina . . . . the Sentinel Pup

Contents

Chapter 1

Leaving

"BossQueen, wake up!" Mina yelped. "Someone's coming."

Chris leaped up and took command. "Layla! Time to bark."

Layla sounded her BigBark as she struggled to her feet, then all three Dogs barked as they ran among the packing boxes to get to the door.

OurShe tried to quiet her Dogs. "Hush, Girls. Everything is okay." But TheGirls had a Job to do and would not settle down, so OurShe put them in the yard until the movers finished, and the van pulled away.

"Did we do a good Job, Chris?" Mina asked.

"Of course we did. They're gone now."

Layla sniffed at the back door and announced, "There are snacks for hungry Dogs."

"Come inside, my good Girls." OurShe set three food bowls on the kitchen floor. Chris and Layla lunged for their meal, but Mina hesitated.

"What's worrying you, Mina?" asked Chris.

"Food is good," Layla said, and crunched a mouthful of kibble.

"But everything's changing." Mina said from a corner. "What if something bad happens?"

"It's just a move."

"OurPack has done it before."

"Not while I've been in it."

"Nothing has changed," Chris said. "We still have OurJob to do. We must watch, guard, and keep the house and everything in it safe."

"OurPack is together. This is good." Layla licked Mina's ear, as if comforting a little pup.

Mina winced. She was not a pup anymore, but the older Dogs did not seem to notice. Soon Layla left her alone and plopped down in the middle of the floor.

"I will be here if you need me to bark." She closed her eyes.

"Should I check Lookouts?" Mina asked Chris.

"Don't bother with them right now. Soon you will have new Lookouts in our new house. But do Pay Attention."

"To what?"

"OurShe, of course. She gives the signals. You must learn them. Watch her closely. When she touches the car keys and our harnesses, it's time to go."

Mina looked from Chris to OurShe. Nothing happened. OurShe continued to place things in bags and take them to the car.

"Chris," asked Mina, "will this move be as long as a ride to the big yard where we play RunningChasing Games? I like that place, but I don't like the long car ride."

"This will be longer."

"What? Longer than that?"

"Yes. Moves can be far away."

OurShe picked up her keys, knelt in front of Chris, and rubbed her ears. "Oh, Chrissy, my dear old Girl, you ready to go? Time to tell the others."

"That is the signal," Chris said to Mina. Chris trotted up and down the room and barked, "Let's go, Girls!"

Layla woke from her nap and rose to her feet. Mina darted from OurShe to the door and back again.

TheGirls arranged themselves before OurShe according to TheOrder of Things. Chris, OurShe's First Dog, nosed into her harness and leash. Then OurShe placed the next harness and leash on Layla, the Second Dog, who wagged her tail all the while. But Mina cringed. She could not understand why the other Girls were always so eager to wear the harnesses, especially on a day like today, with so many changes.

Chris led the way out the door with a slow, rolling gait, her plumed tail swishing as she walked. At the car she waited for OurShe to help her into the back. She was the Queen after all, and Queens, especially plump ones, deserve to be lifted into cars.

As the Second Dog in TheOrder of Things, Layla followed Chris. She limp-skipped on her stiff back legs.

"I am ready! I am following you, Chris!"

Layla, because of her achy hips, deserved to be helped into the car, too.

Mina, the Last Dog in TheOrder of Things, jumped easily into the back.

"TheGirls are in and ready to go," Chris announced. She wagged her tail to let OurShe know that all was well.

Layla wagged her tail, too. "OurShe brought our food bowls. This is good! Anything to eat now? A little snack for hungry Dogs?"

"Will it be a long time before we can get out to play games?" Mina moaned.

OurShe started the car.

"This window will be my Lookout," said Chris as she pushed her nose out the small opening at the top. "Layla, where will you be if I need you to bark?"

"Right here," Layla said as she thudded down in a small space in the back of the car.

"Mina, are you Paying Attention?" snapped Chris.

"What?" Mina's pointed black ears lifted. "I...I'm always Paying Attention. It's what I'm supposed to do, right?"

As the car pulled out onto the road, Chris took up her Lookout position by the window, Layla took up most of the space in the back of the car, and Mina took up worrying.

🐕 Chris's Tale

I love riding in the car! I love the smells! I stick my nose out the window and breathe it all in.

Layla is asleep, and Mina is moping. I lean over the seat and lay my chin on OurShe's shoulder. She reaches back to pet me.

"Good old Chrissy. Another move, you and me. This will be our best yet."

Because I am the BossQueen, OurShe relies on me to make sure everything goes smoothly. I understand about moves. OurShe and I have made many in the long time we have been together.

Unlike Layla, who was given to OurShe, and Mina, who was found by OurShe, I chose to be with OurShe.

When I was a young Dog, I sniffed her and knew that she was the good She I was looking for. I had sniffed others, some who had Dogs, some that did not. Of course, I skipped those with cats. And I could tell by sniffing that some were not good to Dogs. Their yards smelled bad, and their Dogs had nothing to do but yap all day. That is no Job for a Dog.

When I found OurShe, I knew she would need a new Dog soon. Maxie, her Only Dog, was well cared for but was getting old. So I chose to join their Pack. Maxie taught me how to Pay Attention and do TheJob of Dog. Now I have been with OurShe longer than Maxie was.

After Maxie died, I was the Only Dog on TheJob. I became the BossQueen when OurPack grew to include Layla, then Mina. I watch for OurShe's signals and pass them on to TheGirls. Each has her part of TheJob, and I make sure it gets done.

As we drive, Layla sleeps, Mina turns circles in the back of the car, and OurShe tells me about the move. I Pay Attention.

"Chris," she says, "There will be more of us now. You will have a bigger Job. But I am sure you are up to it, my good old Dog."

I swish my tail.

"But," she continues, "you must tell the others: TheGirls can't chase the cat."

Cat? What cat? We have never invited a cat to be with us before.

"That cat already lives in our new house. It's important. You Girls cannot chase their pet."

Getting rid of cats is part of a Dog's Job. Does Our-She really mean that she does not want us to continue to do that part of OurJob? She must be mistaken. We are so good at chasing them away. Dogs and cats do not belong in the same house and yard. When TheGirls move in, cats leave. That cat will also disappear. No uninvited cat. Only three good Dogs.

I wag my tail and lick at OurShe's face to show her that she does not have to worry. The BossQueen is on TheJob. She tells me to lie down, but first I must check the Lookout. I sniff out the window for any danger to OurPack. All is well, but there is something else. Ah, I smell cows! I wish I had the chance to sort them, gather them, and chase them. If I had a herding Job, I would make an excellent Lead Dog.

Layla does not understand about cows. Neither does Mina. But I do. All Australian Shepherds long to be around cows. It would be wonderful if this move took us near them.

Once, when I was younger and was OurShe's Only Dog, we took a Long Walk next to a field full of cows. I crossed the fence and herded them. I used to try to herd OurShe when we walked, but there was only one of her, so we always got tangled up when I played Heel Dog behind her. When I played Lead Dog, I got too far ahead. With the large herd of cows, I had plenty of animals to move around and could show off my natural skill. But soon, OurShe called me back.

"Those are not our cows. No more running under the fence. Stay with me." Then she added, "How does a city pup like you know about herding? You are a smart Dog, Chrissy."

I could tell she was not mad at me but proud of what I could do. And I have wished to be around cows ever since. I bark to tell OurShe this move should include cows. But no cats.

Layla's Tale

The car stops. We wake up. Did we sleep a long time? We must have. Because when we get out of the car to make Puddles and drink water, I need to do both. Badly. What a relief.

We get back in the car while OurShe goes inside the place that smells like good things to eat. I drool waiting for food, but Chris tells us it is time to do TheJob. We guard the car like it is OurHouse. Chris watches the people nearby. I watch Chris. Mina watches everything.

"Alert! Alert!" says Mina, the Sentinel Pup. That Mina has been worrying all day, but now she has something real to worry about. Someone is too near our car!

We do not like this. Chris warns the Someone that TheGirls are on TheJob. Now she tells me it is my turn. I stand up and bark-and-bark-and-bark-and-bark-and-bark-and-bark-and-bark-and-bark-and-bark-and-bark.

I fill the car with barks.

That Someone goes away. But I keep barking.

Here comes OurShe. We have done OurJob, and OurShe can see that we have. We wag our tails. The car is safe. OurPack is safe.

I sniff something yummy. Any food for good Dogs, hungry little Dogs? I push my nose against the bag of food. But OurShe tells us it is food only for her. Not for Dogs.

I am Little BigBark. I am Second Dog. Chris is First. Mina is the youngest and the last to join OurPack. This is TheOrder of Things—Chris, me, then Mina. It is also the order in which we came to OurShe. I know because Chris was there when I came, and I was there when Mina came. Chris is our boss. Mina is our sentinel. And I bark.

Everyone thinks my bark is big. If it is, it is the only big thing about me. I may be the littlest Dog, but I try not to disappoint anyone. I do not hear as well as I once did, or get around as well. But I can still do my Job. I can bark.

OurShe feeds us, pets us, and decides about things like moves. That is her Job. She is bigger than us. I like to get into OurShe's lap whenever I can. To let her know, I put my front paws on her lap, then try and crawl up with my back legs, which sometimes ache too much to push. I put my face to OurShe's face and ask her to lift me up all the way. Usually she does not. I do not get to sit in her lap, where I love to be. OurShe says I do not belong in laps.

The vet says I am small for a Rottweiler. He says that I am only ninety pounds, which proves I am quite little. So why can't I be in her lap?

Most days we guard OurHouse, but today we are moving to a new house. Chris said something about a cat. We hate cats.

Chris and I are good at chasing them. Very good. She herds them toward me, and I hunt them. They escape over or under the fence, and they do not come back. OurYard never has cats. Not with Chris and me around.

Once, long before Mina came to OurPack, Chris and I visited a farm. Chris wanted to find cows to herd, but instead, we found chickens! What fun! Chris sent those fat, flapping birds my way, and I snapped at them. There were dust and feathers and squawking and barking and squawking and dust and feathers and more barking. Soon, OurShe ran over to see what we were doing. Was she ever surprised! She did not know we were so good at herding and hunting! We did not stay long on that farm.

If a cat lives at the new house, we can take care of it just like we took care of those chickens. And this time we have Mina to help. Even better. Three Dogs against one cat. It will not have a chance.

The day is over. The car stops. We make Puddles again; then we go into a one-night house, which has lots and lots of rooms, but we only go into one. TheGirls sniff up the entire room. It is small, and it has lots of different smells. Chris lets OurShe know TheGirls will bark if Someone passes by the door, but OurShe says, "Hush."

Then OurShe feeds us! She brought our food bowls! That makes us happy. Chris eats. I eat. But Mina does not. I do not know why. Eating is so good.

After the food is gone, I sleep.

Mina's Tale

I cannot sleep. I am worried. The smells are all wrong and strange. The sounds are all wrong and strange. I listen and watch all night.

Oh, oh, let's go back home before something bad happens. Moving means everything is different. TheGirls do not understand. If I tell my worries to Chris, she will just sniff at me like I am foolish, but I am not. If I tell my worries to Layla, she will lick me like I am a little pup, but I am not. I worry because I know something they do not.

When morning arrives at last, OurPack gets back in the car. It is noisy, and I do not like the sights going by fast, then slow, then fast again. So much is going on at once it makes my Job as sentinel difficult. I watch in all directions, but it is hard to do with TheGirls in the way. I hate the car.

Most of all, I hate Busy Places. Sometimes something bad happens at those places where cars run back and forth. Dogs can get hurt and worse—lost!

Oh, oh, now I said it. Getting lost is something that has never happened to Chris or Layla. They have always been with OurShe, but I have not. I remember a time before I was one of TheGirls—when I was lost at a Busy Place.

I was taken on a Long Walk. At the end of it, my leash was removed, and I was chased away. Why was I uninvited? What did I do? Where was I to go?

Rain started to fall, and because of it, I could not sniff my way back. Cars darted all about. I dodged and ran between them so they would not hurt me. But as they passed, water splashed all over me. I ran on and on. I huddled under the first shelter that kept me away from cars and out of the rain.

It stormed for a long time. I have not liked thunderstorms ever since. I crept out of the shelter between showers, and though some people fed me and some people petted me, no one took me to their house. Maybe it was because I am just a plain Dog, not any particular breed. I am too big to be a little Dog and too little to be a big Dog. My coat is just black and very short. My ears are short, too, and my tail is just a stub. But I am a good Dog who is nice to everyone, and I am good at Running-Chasing Games. But there were no games when I was lost. I was nobody's special pet.

When OurShe found me, I was cold and wet and sick from the scraps I had eaten. She put a blanket around me and lifted me into her car. She petted me and talked softly to me as we rode. By the time the car stopped at her house, I was warm and not so afraid to be someone's Dog again.

Then I met TheGirls. Clearly they were bosses of a good house and a good She. And they tried to bark me away. I had to act fast so they would not attack me. I am not as heavy as Chris or as huge as Layla. So I did the only thing a clever Dog could do—I put up my hackles and growled, "I am tough and willing to fight, if I must." Then I flipped over on my back like a puppy and said, "But you do not need to bully me. I am clever enough to understand TheOrder of Things. You are the bosses. I will be the Last Dog, if only you will let me stay."

This satisfied the BossQueen. And of course, the Second Dog agreed. After a good sniffing, they invited me to join TheGirls. I became the Last Dog in TheOrder of Things, and the sentinel.

Now more than ever, my part of TheJob is important. Chris and Layla are getting old. They cannot move, or hear, or see as well as a Dog should. I would never tell them so, but they cannot do TheJob without me.

I liked our last house. I was used to the Lookouts, the smells, and the sounds. I hope we can go back there if OurPack does not like this new house.

I do not want anything bad to happen. What if one of OurPack gets lost or uninvited on this move? OurPack would change.

TheGirls do not understand my worries. To them I am just the sentinel and a pup—and last when it comes to anything important.

Chapter 2

Arriving

"Our new house," Chris announced as she strode up the walkway, nose in the air. Were those cows she sniffed? Perhaps, but the BossQueen had no time to pause. She had a Job to do. "Come on, Girls. Everyone inside."

"We are here. At last." Layla climbed stiffly out of the back of the car and followed Chris up the steps into the kitchen.

"Can we get these harnesses and leashes off now?" Mina asked. She waited while OurShe removed the harnesses in order, first Chris, then Layla, then her.

"Oh, that feels so much better." Mina wiggled.

"Now, Girls," Chris commanded. "It is OurJob to learn about this new house. So let's get busy sniffing. We must discover everything."

"I sniff something familiar," Layla said.

"I know!" Mina bounced up and down. "It smells like He! But how can that be?"

"Pay Attention," said Chris. "OurShe said He has invited us into his house. Now, his house becomes OurHouse, and He becomes OurHe."

"He becomes part of OurPack?" asked Layla, giving her tail a small wag.

"Oh, yes, I like that. I like that He!" Mina leaped about as TheGirls continued to sniff. "Oh, oh, I like this move! Nothing bad happened. This house looks like a good house, right Chris?"

"Keep sniffing. And tell me what you find." Chris and Layla headed back to the kitchen.

"I'm sure all is well," Mina said. She dashed around the house.

Chris decided to post herself in the kitchen by the see-through door where she could look outside. Layla decided to post herself in the middle of the kitchen floor where it was warm.

"My new Lookout will be right here," Chris announced and placed her bulk squarely before the entrance. "Where will you be, Layla, in case I need you to bark?"

"Is it okay with you if I lie—I mean, guard—this spot?" Layla asked. She lay down with a thud.

"And what about you, Mina?" Chris asked. "Have you found many good Lookouts? What did you sniff?"

Mina crept into the room. Her tail did not know whether to wag or droop.

"I sniffed two things. One was good, but the other was not."

"Tell me," said Chris.

"The Boy and the Girl live here. I found their bedrooms."

"Are they going to join OurPack?" Layla asked.

"But," said Mina, "there's a cat in this house, too. Is it invited?"

"OurShe told me about it," said Chris.

"We will get that cat," Layla growled. "We will hunt it." She rose to her full height. "We will chase it, so it will not come back. That is what good Dogs do."

"But if we chase away a cat who is invited, will that make us bad Dogs?" Mina worried. "Oh, oh! And this move was going so well!"

🐕 Chris's Tale

I am just deciding what TheGirls should do about the cat, when our new He comes in. We crowd around the door with our special greetings-to-you-we-are-happy-you-are-here bark. It is OurJob now that He is part of OurPack.

After petting us, OurHe opens the door wide, and in come lots of Someones carrying boxes and boxes. TheGirls bark and bark, as all our things are brought in. It is so crowded with boxes, we hardly have room to run around and watch and bark at all those Someones in OurHouse. It is a lot of work, and it takes all of us to do TheJob.

"Hush, Girls. Everything is okay," OurShe says as she sends us out into our new yard.

We stay OnAlert and sniff the yard for Lookouts. From the fence corner I can see the Someones carrying more things into OurHouse. I watch until they go away.

Now that they are gone, I think about chasing the cat.

🐕 Layla's Tale

It is nice to be here in our new yard. There are lots of places to make Puddles. OurShe brings us our water dishes. Will you bring us our food dishes, too? And a snack? For little hungry Dogs?

OurShe tells me to wait.

OurHe joined OurPack today. He has a Boy and a Girl in his Pack, but they are not here now.

Neither is the cat. We would hunt it if it were.

 *Mina's Tale*

OurShe's and OurHe's things are all jumbled together, strange and familiar side by side. TheGirls remember when He visited us at our other house. Whenever He came, He petted us and told us we were good Dogs. We missed him when He left, and TheGirls wanted to invite him into OurPack. I think OurShe did, too. Maybe she did invite him. Or He invited us. Either way, Chris says we are now one Pack. We are glad about this. But we have never been to his house before.

Oh, oh, have I found all the Lookouts here? I worry because if I cannot see or hear what is going on, I will not be able to alert TheGirls to danger. I run from Lookout to Lookout to be sure I can see and hear well from all of them. That is how I made the two discoveries: the bad one about a cat living here, and the good one about the Boy and the Girl living here, too. But why aren't they here now? I wish they were because they were so much fun when they visited our other house. We played lots of RunningChasing Games. This new bigger yard is even better for that, plus there is a field to explore behind the gate. I cannot wait until the Boy and the Girl get here.

"Oh, Chris," I ask, "can they be ours?"

"Of course. Everything in OurHouse is ours."

"Oh, joy, joy!"

"But," Chris cautions, "I sniff that they don't live here all the time."

"Why not?"

Chris just scratches at a patch of dirt.

I wonder where they go when they are not here. Why do they go somewhere else? Do they get uninvited? Do they belong to another Pack? But how can that be?

"If the Boy and the Girl are not here all the time, are they still part of OurPack?"

"Of course." Chris lies down and spreads out on the cool, fresh earth. "We are not just TheGirls and OurShe anymore. You must be OnAlert for the Boy and the Girl. And OurHe. But still Pay Attention to OurShe, because she gives the signals."

I dart around the yard and look for any sign of the Boy and the Girl, but they have not been here for a few days.

But the cat has. Where is it now? What will happen when it returns and finds that TheGirls have moved in? I am afraid Chris wants to hunt it with Layla. The cat is not safe here anymore.

Chapter 3

Settling In

"Oh, oh!" said Mina, skittering into the kitchen.

"What is it?" The BossQueen's head snapped up. She had been resting but now she was fully alert.

"Oh, oh, I think it is…"

"Me-e-e-n-a-a-a-a!" wailed Layla, who had been sleeping in the middle of the floor. "Stop rushing about. You woke me up."

"Yes, but, but…"

"What is it?" Chris interrupted.

"Listen!" Mina ran to the door and tilted her head. Chris and Layla strained their old ears.

"If it is important," Chris huffed, "tell us so we can do OurJob."

"Job? Is it time for me to bark?" Layla glanced anxiously toward the BossQueen.

"Yes! Yes!" the Sentinel Pup called.

"Bark, Layla!" The BossQueen declared. "Bark!"

Little BigBark barked her best go-away-TheGirls-are-on-TheJob bark.

"No!" Mina cried. "Not that kind of bark!"

"But Someone is approaching OurHouse!" Chris called in alarm. "No, two Someones!"

"I am barking!" Little BigBark said, a little panicked. "Oh, joy! Joy!"

Chris and Layla stopped barking. "What? Joy? Joy? What are you saying? This is danger! Two Someones are near OurHouse!"

"Yes, yes! They are! They are here!"

Then Chris knew. "Well, why didn't you say so, Mina?"

"Say so about what? Who is coming?" Layla cried. "Wait! I know!"

Together TheGirls barked out an extra-special greetings-to-you-we-are-happy-you-are-here bark to the Boy and the Girl as they arrived at the kitchen door.

🐕 Chris's Tale

It is my Job to greet them at the door and tell them all is well. Layla, and especially Mina, are so excited they squeeze as close to the door as they can. I try to sort out TheOrder of Things, but everyone is so piled together it is hard to do.

Mina leaps over and around to greet them because they play RunningChasing Games with her. She likes to be a frisky Dog with them.

Layla would like the chance to be their lap Dog, but they are all about the same size so it does not work out too well. The Boy and the Girl do not mind. When they sit together, they let Layla cuddle between them. She wiggles and whines like she did when she was a small pup on OurShe's lap. Back then, Layla was sickly and had to be fed smelly medicine until she got better. Even though she is no longer sick or a pup, she still loves the comfort of laps. So she is happy to see the Boy and the Girl again. I can tell OurShe likes the Boy and the Girl too because she greets them like members of OurPack. I have known OurShe a long time, and she has never invited others to join us before. They must be special to her.

🐕 Layla's Tale

There is lots of greeting and wagging and patting and smiling and patting and greeting and wagging and more smiling. They are small, not big like OurShe. Or OurHe. So they are like me. Maybe I like them so much because we are almost the same size. They think I am big. But I look into their faces and say, "See, you are bigger than me, but if you need me to be big to protect you from danger, I will be. I am good at barking and will bark my best for you."

OurShe invites them in and tells us Dogs to move away from the door. Which we do, because we want them in OurHouse, too. I can tell OurShe likes them, because OurShe feeds and pets them, just like she feeds and pets us. This is good. She tells everyone, Dogs included, to sit down. Then she brings out food for all of us! I put my head on the table and look at their food, but OurShe tells me to eat my food. I like my food, and I will gladly share my food with them. Will they gladly share their food with me? I hope so. Food is good!

When the food is gone, I ask if I can crawl up on their laps. Okay. They sit side by side so I can be on both of their laps at once. Oh, thank you, thank you. I like that ever so much. They pet me from my head to my tail. Can I stay here? It is so warm and cozy. Please? But OurShe says Dogs off the furniture.

🐕 Mina's Tale

Tonight, we celebrate. There are food and games, funny toys and silly hats—even for Dogs. Chris wears her hat like a crown. OurShe says, "Good Dog, Chrissy" over and over, and the Boy and the Girl laugh and clap their hands. Under the brim of her hat, Layla's brow wrinkles and unwrinkles. But she forgets about wearing something on her head when the Boy and the Girl feed her bits of cake. As for me, I cannot, just cannot, wear my hat. They plead and try to clamp it on, but it feels like a harness around my ears. I dodge out of it again and again. To make up for it, I chase bouncing balls, pounce on squeaky Dog Toys, play tug-of-war with a knotted rope, dance through confetti, and wag my stub tail. If I were a licking Dog, which I am not because I am too polite, I would kiss them. Well, maybe I do in all the excitement.

At the end of the party, TheGirls are given presents. Even before the packages are opened we can sniff the brand-new chew bones inside. We jump about until we are given our treats.

When TheGirls settle down to gnaw, I ask Chris, "What are we celebrating?"

"Isn't it obvious?" she says as she chews her bone. "Today we became a new Pack. He and his Boy and Girl joined us and became OurHe, OurBoy, and OurGirl."

"That's good."

"Yes, it is good." Layla crunches her snack. "Best bone I ever had."

"No, Layla. Mina means it is good to be in a new Pack."

The only reply is Layla's chomping and slurping.

"You know, Mina, bigger Job, more work," Chris says.

"More fun," I say, "with more petting and more games."

She sniffs at me like I am foolish, but I am not. I understand that much has changed. Is that a problem for TheGirls? Maybe the cat is now part of the new Pack and our bigger Job. But he can't be. He was not invited to celebrate with us. I decide not to worry about it. Tonight has been a happy night.

Chapter 4

The Dogs of
the Neighborhood

The party was over, and TheGirls trotted outside into their new yard to make Puddles before bedtime. Suddenly every Dog in the neighborhood knew The-Girls had moved in!

"Hey, you!" they barked.

"Hey, you!" TheGirls barked back.

"We are here," they said.

"We are here, too," TheGirls said.

"Yeah?"

"Yeah!"

"You can't come into my yard!"

"You can't come into my yard!"

"Fine."

"Fine."

"Hey, who are you anyway?"

"We are TheGirls. BossQueen! Little BigBark! And the Sentinel Pup! This is now OurHouse."

"Yeah?" they said. "You are in That Cat's house."

"What? There is no cat here!"

"Of course there is. He is out on a long prowl. But you will meet him because you live in his house."

"This is OurHouse! And no cat is going to live here!"

"But one does. Or haven't you heard? Cats live where they decide to live. And That Cat decided to live there."

"We can get rid of a cat."

"Other cats, maybe. But you do not know That Cat. That Cat thinks he belongs wherever he pleases. He will sit where he wants to sit—even if it is your Lookout. He will eat what he wants to eat—even if it is your food. He will be First in TheOrder of Things— even if it is your Pack!"

"No! No! No!" TheGirls barked furiously. "We are good cat hunters. This will not happen in OurHouse—to OurPack!"

OurShe rushed out into the yard. "Chris! Layla! Mina! Hush. What's all the fuss? Come back inside, at once!"

TheGirls, who were good Dogs, turned to go, but the Dogs of the Neighborhood called after them, "Just you wait. When That Cat comes back, you will see."

"No. *You'll* see."

Chris climbed the steps with her nose held high. "What silly Dogs."

"Yeah," Layla said, limping up after her. "What kind of Dogs are afraid of a cat?"

"What kind of cat makes Dogs afraid?" Mina wondered, shivering as she looked back into the cold night sky.

Chapter 5

Meeting That Cat

"Cat!" barked the BossQueen.

"Cat!" barked Little BigBark.

"Oh, oh!" Mina halted just inside the kitchen door.

That Cat was in OurHouse! In the kitchen! Chris and Layla rushed at it and barked their get-the-cat bark, but That Cat flew, yes flew, up the wall and landed on top of the kitchen window, knocking over dishes, papers, and the curtain rod.

As That Cat flew by her, Mina wondered, "How do cats do that? Where do they keep their wings?"

Such a commotion! TheGirls barked, OurShe yelled, and then That Cat disappeared. Cats can do that. Mina saw him get narrow, the way cats can but Dogs cannot, and slip through the tiny opening in the door.

"Where is That Cat?" Chris and Layla cried as they sniffed, hunted, and begged for That Cat.

"It disappeared," Mina said.

"We know! We know! But where?"

But how could Mina explain what she had seen? She did not quite understand it herself. Besides, there was such a stir going on around her, she could not stop and wonder about it. But she was certain of one thing: That Cat had tricks.

🐕 *Chris's Tale*

That Cat! That Cat was in OurHouse! TheGirls chased him—chased him out of the kitchen. We did a good Job of getting rid of him.

But That Cat did not know it! He has not left. The nerve of him! He is just outside the see-through door. We can see him parade right in front of us! We cannot get to him. The cheater! We bark and push and squeeze one another to get closer, to let him know he is in danger from TheGirls. He is lucky we cannot break through the door, because we know how to hunt cats. Give us a fair chance, and we will chase him away forever.

But does that scare That Cat? No. Instead, he fluffs out his tail and paces slowly by, as if he cannot hear us or does not care.

Now he glares straight at us.

"My, my, such a racket," he purrs, like he is not upset at all. "Oh. Did you think you had frightened me away? What nonsense. I left because you are so loud and make such a fuss, not because I thought you might catch me. You are just three fat old dogs, and I am a fine tomcat in his prime. I am not ruled by you. Dogs do not concern me."

"Leave OurHouse," I demand.

"Your house? You think this is your house? We'll see about that."

"Let's see about it now."

"Or later. I will be out for the evening, but I will be back. This is not over yet."

"Well, that is one thing we agree upon, Cat," I growl. "This is not over."

Soon he may find out how well Layla and I can hunt.

Layla's Tale

That Cat is big! And fast! I am glad I was not alone. Not that I am afraid of cats. We scare cats. Chris herds them toward me, and I hunt them. Usually they run off. But That Cat is sort of fierce—and sassy. I hope TheGirls chase him away for good. Most cats do not come back.

But this one did.

I do not like cats, especially big sassy cats who keep coming back.

Mina's Tale

"Of course I saw what he looks like!" Chris snaps. "And if I see That Cat around again, I will bark at him until he knows who is boss around here. He cannot escape now that I know what he looks like."

She did not hear me correctly. What I said was, "Did you see how That Cat looked at us?" But the Boss-Queen and Little BigBark do not want to hear what I have to say. So I wander into the room with the soft carpet to be by myself.

Chris and Layla want to hunt him like they have hunted cats before. They want to show me how, so I can join them, but I do not want to. I do not think TheGirls should hunt That Cat. But they do not listen to me because I am the Last Dog. If they did, I would tell them that they are not as quick as they once were. I would also tell them That Cat has more tricks than they know. He has wings to fly, and he can get narrow to go through small spaces, which may mean he has other tricks, too.

I think the Dogs of the Neighborhood know something about That Cat that we do not. He does not look like the kind of cat who can be bullied by anyone. Chris is smart, but she does not see that we do not frighten That Cat. He might stay, even without the BossQueen's consent.

That Cat looked at me, Layla, and yes, even Chris, with a look that said, "I am tough and can fight. Do not even think of making me Last in TheOrder of Things. I will stay as I am—boss of this house."

Oh, how can I explain that to the BossQueen? There cannot be two bosses. It is not TheOrder of Things. But if TheGirls get rid of That Cat, won't that make us bad? Bad Dogs are uninvited, right? Will TheGirls have to move again, or will OurShe take us on a Long Walk and leave us at a Busy Place? Oh, please, I do not want to be lost again.

Chapter 6

Something in the House

OurBoy and OurGirl patted and hugged TheGirls, then climbed into bed.

"Good night," they said.

TheGirls settled down on the rug at the foot of Our-She's and OurHe's bed. Everyone was tired after such a long day, and they all soon fell asleep—except Mina. Her sharp ears picked up the sound of scuttling in the kitchen.

"Chris?"

"Humph, humph. Cows. Where are the cows?"

"No cows, Chris. It's me, Mina. Wake up."

"Why? What's wrong? Is Someone near OurHouse? Should I get Layla to bark?"

"No. Yes. I mean…maybe…I don't know. I think I hear Something in the kitchen. Do you?"

Chris strained her old ears. "It's probably nothing. You are just not used to the sounds of this house yet." She rested her head on her paws. Suddenly she snapped up again. "It's not That Cat, is it?"

"No, I'm sure of that."

"Good." Chris relaxed. "Well, you stay OnAlert. When you are certain about the Something, let me know." She yawned and was asleep before Mina could say okay.

Mina pricked up her ears, but all was quiet. Was the Something gone?

"Maybe Chris is right. I am just not used to all the new sounds in this house." She tried not to worry. When she finally closed her eyes, she slept fitfully.

Bang!

What was that?

Mina awoke with a start. Early morning light came faintly in the window.

"Mina! Get in here!" OurHe called from the kitchen. Mina and the BossQueen arrived in an instant.

Layla remained in the bedroom, where she struggled to lift herself out of sleep and up from the carpet.

"What happened? What's going on?" Mina dashed from OurShe to OurHe to Chris and back again.

"Where's the cat when we need him?" OurShe fussed.

"Cat?" Mina asked. "Why do we need him?"

"Be quiet, Mina," said Chris. "This is OurJob now. Pay Attention."

"What Job?"

"Something's in there," Chris quivered as she stared at an overturned bucket in the center of the kitchen floor. "OurHe dropped that bucket over it and trapped it."

"Oh, oh, I recognize those sounds underneath there. That's what woke me up. That is the same Something I heard last night!"

"You never told me you heard a mouse in Our-House!" Chris would have snapped at Mina, but she did not take her eyes off the bucket for an instant.

"I did tell you. Remember, I woke you up? What's a mouse? I heard it, but you didn't believe me. Is it big? Should we get Layla to bark at it?"

"No, I will take care of it. Pay Attention." She lunged for the bucket, but OurHe's firm grip stopped her.

"Chris, you fat old Dog," OurHe said. "Let Mina take care of it. She's quicker, and we'll probably only get one chance at this."

"Chance? What chance?" Mina trembled. "Am I supposed to do something?"

OurShe lifted the bucket. Chris strained hard against OurHe's arms. Mina fidgeted, afraid of what she would see. Under the bucket, curled up and shaking, was a tiny creature no bigger than a Dog Toy.

Just then Layla shuffled in blinking the sleep from her eyes. "What is going on?"

OurHe reached out a hand to stop her from startling the mouse. But it was too late! The mouse made a sudden dash to escape. Chris broke from OurHe and leaped onto the mouse as spryly as a pup. Before anyone else could make a move, she had it in her jaws and shook it from side to side. She harried it and tossed it about until the mouse remained still.

"So that's what you do," Mina said.

"About what?" Layla's brow furrowed.

"A mouse," Chris said as the little limp thing dropped from her mouth to the floor.

OurHe clapped his hands and laughed. "Who would've thought old Chris could move so quickly?"

"Good Dog, Chrissy! Good Dog!" OurShe said.

"Were you Paying Attention, Mina?" Chris asked.

"Sure." Mina stared at the mouse.

"Now you try."

"Try what? You want me to put that in my mouth?"

"Can I have it?" Layla went over to sniff it. "I want to play with it a little."

"I was not playing. I was getting rid of it. It does not belong in OurHouse. But," Chris said, "if you want it, you will have to claim it before OurShe or OurHe does."

OurHe got out a broom and dustpan from the closet. Layla scooped up the mouse in her huge jaws, but immediately OurHe asked for it back.

"Drop it, Layla."

Layla edged toward the living room, her eyes pleaded with Chris to let her keep the prize.

"Fine," Chris said, "but leave it where OurHe can find it when you are done."

Layla dashed away with the mouse.

"Where do you think you're going?" OurHe followed, broom in hand. "I really don't want to have to reach into your mouth. Come on, Layla. Give it back. Now!"

🐕 Chris's Tale

Today we got rid of a mouse. Mina did not know what it was or what to do about it. I showed her. I hope she remembers what to do from now on. It is so hard to train a pup.

I think about Maxie, my Lead Dog. She was so patient and kind as she taught me about being a good Dog, about TheJob, and about OurShe. I caught on quickly, which was good, because Maxie left so soon. I hope Mina will learn all there is to know from me before it is my time to go.

Enough! Or I will be worrying like Mina herself.

At least today we proved we do not need That Cat. Now we can hunt it away. I will teach Mina how.

🐕 Layla's Tale

A Dog Toy! I toss and toss and toss it again. But it does not run like it did for Chris. I guess she took all the play out of it.

OurHe asks for it back. Sure, you can have it, but it will not play for you either.

OurHe takes it into the field behind OurYard. I want to sniff for it.

But OurHe says, "No! Stay!"

So I wait behind the gate and watch as OurHe digs a hole. TheGirls could help with that. Then OurHe puts the mouse inside the hole and covers it up. He thinks he is hiding it from us, but Dogs can sniff things under the ground and can dig them up later. Ooo, I hear OurShe putting food on the table! Any food for me? A small snack for hungry Dogs? Just a little bite?

🐕 Mina's Tale

So that was the Something I heard last night. I was right to try and alert Chris about it. Now I know what to do next time.

I do not understand why TheGirls have to get rid of Something so small. OurShe and OurHe do not want it here. Neither does Chris. But it is so tiny, what can it do? Can it hurt OurPack? Oh, oh, I do not want it to hurt anyone! For OurPack, I would become a mouse hunter. But luckily I do not have to because Chris is here to do that Job.

Chapter 7

Meeting That Cat Again

OurShe, OurHe, and the children waved good-bye and left TheGirls in charge of guarding the house. The BossQueen positioned herself at her Lookout, where she could watch the front door. She also sniffed for passing neighborhood children, and every so often she caught a whiff of cows in the distance, which stirred her Shepherd nature. Layla stretched out behind Chris, ready in case her big bark was needed. Mina ran like a black blur from Lookout to Lookout and checked that everything was safe.

"All is well," she told Chris.

"Good," Chris said, without turning toward her.

Mina waited for instructions, but when none came, she lay down next to TheGirls.

"Chris, what are we going to do about That Cat?" she asked.

Chris pulled herself away from the dream of herding cows to the thought of hunting cats. "I think we can come up with a plan."

"What do you mean?"

"That Cat cannot catch mice, which is the only thing cats are good for. It's the reason they're invited into a house. He failed, and so he should be uninvited. TheGirls can catch mice. Even though That Cat is the sassiest one we have ever met, we could hunt him if you learned to help."

A shiver ran down Mina's spine.

"That would be good," Layla said, yawning. "I like hunting. Let's get That Cat."

"We can plan it after our nap," Chris said. She and Layla stretched out across the kitchen floor and dozed off. Mina curled up, but couldn't go to sleep.

Chris's Tale

OurPack returns, and we are ready with our greetings-to-you-we-are-happy-you-are-here bark. After we tell them all is well and receive our pats, we are sent out into OurYard.

Layla sniffs around for a mouse, even though I tell her she will not find another one. Mina runs with OurBoy and OurGirl. I head for the cool patch of dirt

I have been digging, but OurShe calls me back into OurHouse.

OurShe invites only me, not the other Girls, because I am the BossQueen and deserve special privileges. But not this time, I soon discover. OurShe has another reason for inviting me inside. She kneels and holds me around my neck.

"Be a good Girl," she says. "I want to introduce you to the cat. TheGirls must get along with him."

Why should I get along with him? He will be leaving soon. He does not do his Job.

High up on a ledge That Cat is grooming himself. He stops, stares, and then puffs himself up. At me! The nerve!

"I will not get along with That Cat," I growl low.

"Hush," OurShe says. "You tell the other Girls: no more cat chasing, understand? Thomas is their cat. He belongs here, too."

"No!" I bark. "I am the BossQueen, and he does not do his Job!"

"Chris!" OurShe reprimands me! In front of That Cat! A cat who does not catch mice! It is almost more than I can stand, but I know TheOrder of Things. OurShe is my boss, so I calm myself for her sake.

I grit my teeth but do not growl, "Cat, you will have to do your Job to live in OurHouse."

He squints down at me. "Job? What job?"

"Getting rid of mice, and whatever else cats are supposed to do. You should know TheJob of cat better than I."

"Cats don't have jobs," he scoffs.

"Then what good are you? Why are you invited?"

"I am not 'invited.' I just live here, because I want to." He licks his paw then swipes it across his whiskers.

"Unbelievable! You don't deserve the food you eat."

"Why should you care? I don't eat your food."

"And you can't have it! And you can't sleep in our bedroom."

"Why would I want to? At night, I prowl like a sensible animal."

"I don't want you in the same room with me!"

"I don't care what you want. I do as I please, and I go where I please."

"You can't talk to me like that!"

"Yes, I can. I'll speak to you any way I like."

That does it! I jump at him and bark my fiercest get-the-cat bark. He shows his pointed cat teeth. I leap at him. He humps his back and hisses. I want to get him, but OurShe pulls me back and shoves me outside. The door bangs behind me.

This is no way to treat a Queen!

Layla's Tale

Chris returns mad enough to bite. Mina moves out of the BossQueen's Lookout spot just in time. I ask Chris what is wrong, but she just lifts her nose and turns away.

The cold wind makes my hips ache, so I scratch at the kitchen door to tell OurShe I want to get warm. I am glad when OurBoy opens the door. He goes outside, and I slip in before the door closes. This is good. It is warm in the kitchen. No one else is here, so I can nap.

But first, I sniff around for a little food. My bowl is empty, but there are some crumbs on the table which OurBoy and OurGirl left for me. I find a few more tidbits they left for me on the floor. Then I sniff something on the counter. I am little, but I put my nose up there and find a tiny food bowl. A small snack for hungry Dogs! How about that!

Suddenly That Cat is there! He walks across the counter toward me. Toward my snack! No time to bark for TheGirls. I lunge at That Cat. I am so close, I almost get him when—ow! He gets me! He stabs me! Yowwww! Chris! Mina! I am wounded! Get OurShe, quick!

Am I going to die?

OurShe told us that we are not supposed to get That Cat, but Chris was not around to remind me. I only wanted to chase him away from my snack. I curl up in OurShe's lap for a long time. OurShe pets me and talks to me and rubs cool stuff on my nose, and now it does not hurt—much.

Why did I think I was big enough to hunt That Cat alone? He hurt me with his Dog-stabbing knives.

I will not go near That Cat by myself again. I will not forget.

🐕 Mina's Tale

Layla got a cat scratch, so OurShe takes her to the vet. Chris has to go, too, but I do not know why. She is not scratched. I am told to stay. I am glad, because I sniff rain. Rain makes me want to hide inside the house and curl up until it is over. But OurBoy and OurGirl must like this rain, because they yell and point out the window and say, "Snow! Snow! Come on, Mina!"

We rush outside. They dance around in the drops, which are soft and cold but not wet. Soon I dance with them and snap at the flakes. Afterward, I help them carry sticks inside the house so OurHe can make a fire. Then we are warm again. I curl up on the soft rug beside them and roll over on my back so they can rub my belly. It is wonderful to have them all to myself. I am about to drift off to sleep when my nose alerts me: That Cat has entered the room.

Ears do not detect cats, because cats do not make a sound when they walk. Maybe cats do not touch the ground and that is why my ears do not hear him. But cats do have a smell, so my nose sniffs him right away.

OurBoy reaches out to That Cat.

"Thomas," he calls, "here, kitty, kitty."

That Cat walks over and rubs against OurBoy's hand. I do not move. Maybe he does not know I am here. Cat noses are so small I doubt they can smell anything at all. OurBoy wiggles a stick before That Cat. He stiffens and stares at it. His head jerks as he watches it move. Then his paw shoots out, and he catches it! Up he jumps to land right on top of the stick!

Oh, I love pouncing games. I never knew cats could play. I roll over so I can see better, but That Cat steps back and glares at me.

"I'm not going to chase you," I say. "I'm just watching."

The stick wiggles. That Cat cannot stop himself from looking at it. It wiggles again. He is too distracted to worry about me. He is about to pounce, but I reach out with my paw and trap the stick first.

"So you think you're faster than I at this game?" he challenges.

"Maybe." I do not let on that I am very good at games.

"Okay. Let's see how good you are."

So we play. First he pounces on the stick, then I pounce. OurGirl picks up another stick and begins to wiggle it, too. Now we are pouncing everywhere.

Jump. Pounce. Pounce. Jump. That Cat is mighty agile, but I am better at grabbing and shaking. I do not growl the way I like to when I shake a stick because I might scare him off, and, well, I do not want to because we are having so much fun.

Wait. I hear a car approaching. Suddenly I am OnAlert. I bark, and That Cat flies to the window ledge so fast I missed the chance to see his wings.

"Oops. Sorry, Cat. I didn't mean to scare you. I was just doing my Job."

But it is too late. The game is over.

The car door slams, and I can hear OurShe, Chris, and Layla nearing the kitchen door.

"Can we play another time?" I say before I rush to them with the greetings-to-you-we-are-happy-you-are-here bark.

That Cat turns and stares at me, but his stare does not seem quite so scary anymore.

"Okay," he says. "If you think you can keep up with me."

"You know I can." I grin. And I think he grins, too, but it is hard to tell with cats.

As he heads down the hallway, I say, "Don't tell Chris or Layla."

"Why would I talk to a dog?"

Which is kind of funny because he is talking to me, and I am a Dog. I do not get a chance to point this out though, because TheGirls come in, and That Cat becomes narrow and slips through the crack in the bedroom door. I will have to ask him sometime how he does that—and where he keeps his wings and the other things I want to know about cats.

"How was the vet?" I ask as I dart into the kitchen.

Chris does not answer, but Layla says, "Look what I got."

She lowers her nose so that I can see the bandages on it. I sniff them.

"Good. What did you get, Chris?"

"She got treats," Layla answers for her.

"What kind of treats?"

OurShe pours smelly treats out of a bottle, but Chris does not look like she wants them.

Layla tries to sniff them, but OurShe pushes her aside. "No, Layla. The pills are for Chris."

"Are they good?" Layla asks.

Chris is silent, and she does not eat them even though OurShe tries to put one in her mouth.

"Come on, Chris. You've got to take these." She sighs, then takes out some cheese, cuts it into chunks, and wraps the treats inside one chunk. OurShe gives it to Chris, who eats it in two bites and a swallow.

"Good Dog, my Chrissy. That's a good Girl."

OurShe offers Layla and me the other chunks. We eat them and wag our tails, but Chris just goes to her Lookout, lies down, and puts her head on her paws.

OurShe stoops down and rubs her ears. "Poor old Chris. What a good Dog you are."

"Will you pet me, too?" Layla noses in.

OurShe thumps Layla's sides, but she does not stop looking at Chris. I hear her sigh when she gets up. I wonder what is wrong with OurShe.

Chapter 8

Plans for a Hunt

Soon the smells and sounds of the new house and yard were as familiar to TheGirls as those in the other house had been. They learned where all the best Lookouts, the warmest spots, the coolest drafts, and the softest carpets were. They stayed OnAlert all day and greeted OurHe and OurShe when they returned in the evening. The Dogs learned that the children were part of their Pack one week and part of another Pack the next week.

The children learned to greet Chris first. They knew Layla would snatch any unattended food. They knew Mina would play games with them.

TheGirls enjoyed having a bigger Pack. With OurHe, OurBoy, and OurGirl, there were more pats, more walks, more snacks from more hands under the table.

A bigger Pack was more work, but TheGirls could do TheJob.

The only thing TheGirls wished they had less of was That Cat.

🐕 Chris's Tale

Time to get rid of That Cat. Time to tell Layla to hunt. Time to teach Mina to do that part of TheJob.

This will require a smart plan. When stray cats wander into OurYard, TheGirls just bark and run them off. The cats always leave quickly and never return. Most cats figure out, when Dogs guard a house, they are uninvited.

But not That Cat. He still believes he is invited to live in OurHouse and to eat whenever he wants. But he takes this privilege too lightly. He has forgotten his Job, or he is too lazy to do it after prowling all night. He is not alert enough to catch mice. I am sure OurShe would agree. So once That Cat is gone she will see that I am right and did a good Job.

The hunt is a Dog's Job and must happen when the rest of OurPack will not interfere. The sentinel will tell us where That Cat hides. I will bark him toward Little BigBark, and she will get him. I hope she can do her Job. After That Cat scratched her, Layla has been skittish about cat hunting. But if she cannot, Mina will have to do it for her. Part of guarding OurHouse is getting rid of mice and cats.

Layla or Mina must be quick, because I do not want to herd That Cat far. I ached all day after hunting that mouse. As Queen, I will not complain about the pains my Job causes my old body, but I do notice.

🐕 Layla's Tale

OurShe and OurHe are gone. So are OurBoy and OurGirl.

Chris asks Mina to find That Cat. Mina says he is sleeping in OurGirl's bedroom.

Are we hunting now? I like to hunt. But I am just a little Dog. I do not want to get hurt by That Cat's Dog-stabbing knives again.

Chris says Mina will help. This is good. Mina is a frisky Dog. Maybe she can get That Cat before he gets her. I hope so.

Okay, I am ready. Let's go.

🐕 Mina's Tale

Oh, oh this is bad. TheGirls are hunting That Cat! Chris rushes into OurGirl's bedroom with her get-that-cat bark. Layla barks, too, but she stands outside in the hallway and waits for Chris to chase him toward her. I think Layla does not want to get near those knives.

Chris barks That Cat to the top of a tall bookcase. He arches and glares down at her. Chris places her front paws on the bottom shelf. She would climb up if she could, but she cannot reach him. With That Cat trapped so high up, Layla boldly enters the room, and side by side with Chris snaps and growls.

Didn't OurShe tell us not to hunt That Cat? Why did I tell the BossQueen where he was?

"Hey, you," they shout. "Come down here and learn what Dogs can do."

That Cat pulls his face into a horrible mask of sharp teeth and flattened ears. "Why don't you come up here and learn what a Cat can do?"

Layla throws herself against the bookcase. It rocks back a bit.

Chris calls up to him. "I told you to leave. But you did not listen to the BossQueen. Now you are cornered."

"Cornered? I dare say I can stay up here much longer than you can stay down there. So stay. See if I care."

TheGirls pound against the bookcase. It sways back and forth. Things fall off, but not That Cat. He adjusts to the movement better than a Dog riding in a car.

Chris and Layla knock it again and again. More and more things topple to the ground. I dodge to the side so I will not be hit, but TheGirls are too intent on the hunt to dodge anything.

"Please stop," I say.

A shelf crashes down. TheGirls bolt backward as it tumbles to the floor. With Chris and Layla distracted, and his perch falling apart under him, That Cat glances about for another high refuge. But TheGirls see him get ready to jump.

"Jump, Cat. Jump. We will catch you. Go ahead."

"No, wait," I plead.

That Cat looks toward the window. But it is closed. He cannot flee that way, no matter how narrow he makes himself.

"Where can you run, Cat? We have you now."

They lunge again and cause the bookcase to bang loudly against the wall, and then it starts to tip forward.

"Look out!" I yell.

I leap back into the doorway as the tall bookcase falls forward. Everything on it, except That Cat, crashes to the floor and on top of Chris and Layla. As his perch topples, That Cat jumps toward the door, where he lands right in front of me!

He fixes me with a creepy stare. "Want to play games, dog?"

"N-N-No," I stammer.

"Good. Then I will take my leave." Without moving his eyes away from me he slinks backward out the door. Then he turns, streaks down the hallway, and disappears.

"Ow!" Chris cries. "Get this off me!"

"Yowwww," Layla wails. "That Cat dumped everything on top of us."

TheGirls are trapped under the bookcase, which is leaning partly against the bed. It is not resting on them, but Chris is too round and Layla is too huge to crawl out from under it.

"I'll help." But I do not know how. Just then my ears tell me OurShe is home! I rush to the door, but I do not bark the greetings-to-you-we-are-happy-you-are-here bark.

"All is not well!" I tell her.

"Chris? Layla? Where are you?" she calls.

I show her.

"What happened here?" she cries. "What were you Girls doing?"

Chris tries to explain we were getting rid of That Cat. Layla tries to explain how That Cat trapped them and made everything fall.

OurShe lifts the bookcase and gets Chris and Layla out. She checks to see if they are hurt, tells them they are lucky, and scolds them for making a mess. Then she sends TheGirls outside into the yard. I hear the kitchen door bang shut behind them.

All is quiet.

I do not want her to scold me, so I slip into the bedroom to lie down. I hear a hiss when I enter. That Cat glares at me from the bed.

"So you are a hunter now?" he says.

"No."

"Really? Aren't you going to take over where your bossy queen left off? Do you want Cat marks like those I gave the big hunter?"

"No. But I think you should go. They won't stop, you know."

"Neither will I. This is my place. You dogs will have to learn some new tricks. I have plenty I will gladly teach them. Shall I start with you?"

"No, thanks."

I try to tuck my tail down, but a stub cannot tuck. I creep from the room, glad Chris is not around to see me. She would sniff at me for being foolish. But I am not foolish; I am just not as bossy as she is or as big as Layla.

"There you are, Mina." OurShe finds me in the hallway. "You go outside with the others while I straighten up this mess you Dogs made."

She lets me out, and I trot over to Chris and Layla in the corner of the yard.

"Did TheGirls do a good Job?" I ask.

The BossQueen settles herself further down into her dirt patch. "Of course we did. That Cat will be too scared to stay here now."

"But didn't our hunt upset OurShe?"

Layla licks herself as if tending a wound. "OurShe was mad at That Cat. He made the mess."

"Another reason she will be glad when TheGirls get rid of him," Chris adds.

"What if he stays?"

"We will hunt him again. If you had Paid Attention, we could have gotten him this time."

I droop and go to the gate to wait for OurBoy and OurGirl. I hope they are on their way back to Our-House. I am much better at RunningChasing Games than at hunting.

I wonder if TheGirls really hunt cats as well as they think they do. That Cat is not scared. He did not leave. Chris and Layla insist OurShe and OurHe will be glad once we get rid of him. But OurShe was not glad about the mess in OurGirl's bedroom. Isn't that bad? I do not think we did a good Job. I hope Chris does not plan another hunt. I do not want to be part of it.

Maybe if I were boss, I would understand why That Cat cannot live in a house with Dogs and why he bothers Chris and Layla so much. But as Last Dog, it is not my Job. I am glad. I would rather play games.

Chapter 9

A Short Walk with TheGirls

OurShe called all her Dogs to go for a short walk around the block. Suddenly every Dog of the Neighborhood knew TheGirls were out and about.

"Hey, you!" they barked.

"Hey, you!" TheGirls barked back.

"We are here," they said.

"We are here, too," TheGirls said.

"You can't come into my yard!"

"You can't come into my yard!"

"Fine."

"Fine."

"Hey, how are you getting along in that house?

"Good."

"And That Cat?"

TheGirls were silent.

"Ha," they scoffed. "He's still there, isn't he?"

"We have chased him."

"But he still lives with you."

"He will leave soon."

"What kind of cat hunters are you? You told us you would get rid of That Cat. But you can't, can you? Are you too old, or slow?"

"We aren't too old, or slow. He is fast and sassy, that's all."

"We told you he was tough."

"Besides, OurShe does not like us to hunt."

"Hunt him anyway. You are Dogs," they snapped.

"We must not—," Mina began.

"We will chase him every chance we get," Chris snapped back, straining against her leash. "We can make him leave, even if OurShe says no cat hunting."

"Hush, Girls," said OurShe. "Enough barking! Chris, you're panting. Is this walk too long? Oh, Layla, are your hips hurting? Poor things. Sorry, Mina. You could go on and on, couldn't you, but not these old ladies. Time to go home."

"Hey, you!" The Dogs of the Neighborhood barked as TheGirls passed by again.

"Hey, you!" they replied.

"Will you get uninvited if you hunt That Cat? Where would you live then?"

TheGirls were silent.

"Don't think you can come into my yard," the Dogs of the Neighborhood barked.

"Fine."

"Fine. Just so you know."

Chapter 10

A Long Walk
without TheGirls

"Inside, Girls!" Chris commanded as they finished their walk.

"Good. I am hungry," Layla said, licking her droopy muzzle.

"Hey, they're home!" Mina barked as she bounded up the steps and into the kitchen.

OurBoy and OurGirl sat at the table eating an after-school snack.

"Greetings to you." Chris poked her nose into each one's hand to receive her pats for good Dogs.

"Hello, hello." Layla poked her nose into each one's plate, hoping to receive a snack for hungry Dogs.

Mina followed closely. "It's a great day for RunningChasing Games. Want to go out in the yard with me?" She dashed from OurBoy to OurGirl and back again.

"Come on, Girls," said Chris. "Leave OurBoy and OurGirl alone. OurShe said to go away, and besides, we have a Job to do." Chris trotted to her Lookout to watch for neighborhood children and to sniff for cows, but the short walk had worn her out, and she soon settled down for a nap.

Layla flopped in the middle of the kitchen floor, where she could be found if there were any leftovers.

While Mina made her rounds of all the Lookouts in the house, she heard OurBoy and OurGirl call for her. She raced back to the kitchen, where they had taken her leash and harness off the peg by the door.

🐕 Chris's Tale

I pant to cool off after that Walk when Mina rushes up to me and asks, "Chris? What's going on?"

"They're taking you outside. Isn't that what you asked them to do?" I stretch out on the floor.

"Why do I have to put on the leash and harness just to go in the yard?"

"Don't be silly!" I say. "They're taking you for a Walk. You know the rule—Dogs must be in harnesses and leashes outside the gate. How else will anyone know you belong to a Pack?"

"I know, I know, but you and Layla are coming, too. Right?"

Mina looks over at Layla, but she is already sound asleep.

I lay my head on my paws. "No, we are tired out. Besides, I am not invited. Neither is Layla. You are the only Dog going."

"But I don't want to be. That's not TheOrder of Things," Mina protests. "Something bad might happen if you're not there with me."

"Mina, quit complaining. Be a good Dog and be OnAlert. You know TheJob."

Layla's Tale

"Me-e-e-n-a-a-a-a! Stop whining. You woke me up."

Mina is trembling because OurBoy and OurGirl are putting her in her harness. Why is she complaining? I am the one who was having a wonderful dream.

Good. They are leaving OurHouse. Maybe now I can get back to sleep. In my dream I am lying on my back across two, maybe three laps. Everyone is dropping yummy food into my mouth. Mmmm. Smack. Smack.

More? Do you have more? I like this.

⟪dog icon⟫ *Mina's Tale*

I do not like this. Why aren't the BossQueen and Little BigBark with me? Where are OurGirl and Our-Boy taking me? Have I been bad?

The Dogs of the Neighborhood startle us by barking as we pass their yards. I try not to whimper as I call back, "Hey, remember me? I am one of TheGirls. No need to be OnAlert. I am not coming into your yard."

"Fine. Why are you out without your Pack?"

"I'm being taken on a Walk. I'm afraid because sometimes Dogs get lost on Walks."

"Are you being uninvited because you did a bad Job with That Cat?"

"I don't know."

"If you are, you can't come in my yard."

"I know."

We travel far from the house. This Walk is not just around the block. It is a Long Walk. Where are we going? Sometimes OurBoy holds my leash, sometimes OurGirl. He tugs when he is not Paying Attention, but she is alert and careful. Funny thing, tugs from the leash on a collar kind of hurt, but when I am in a harness, they do not. Maybe this harness is not so bad after all.

We come to a big yard with tall trees and grass. It looks like a good place for RunningChasing Games.

But beside it is a Busy Place with lots of parked cars, and I get a bad feeling. I droop.

Then something bad happens. They take off my leash. It is the end of the Long Walk, and I am being lost. Uninvited again!

Oh, oh, what have I done? Please don't leave me! I am a good Dog. Put my leash back on. I don't mind it, really! Please. I don't want to find a different Pack.

OurBoy and OurGirl head to a dirt path that winds up a hill, but that is not the way back to OurHouse. They turn and call to me to follow them. I worry that they will be lost, too. If they are, I can show them the way home. Even if they do not want me in their Pack anymore, I must still do my Job. I run after them.

This hill is higher than any hill I have walked up before. OurBoy and OurGirl stop and rest. It is harder for them, I think, because they do not have as many legs as I do. Still, they want to go higher, so I go ahead of them like a good Lead Dog and watch over them, even if they are going to leave me soon.

I am sorry. I will try and get along with That Cat. OurShe does not want us to chase him because he is your special pet, isn't he? Even if I am Last Dog I will try to tell the BossQueen and Layla to leave him alone. Just please do not leave me.

"Look!" OurGirl says and points. There is a bench at the top of the trail and a metal railing between the bench and a steep drop-off. Is this where they will leave me? I tremble so much that I almost do not see that we have made it to the top of a mountain.

"We did it!" they exclaim. They pet me and say, "Good Dog, Mina! Good Dog."

Are you saying good-bye? Are you leaving me, now?

OurBoy picks up a stick. Oh, oh, please, don't hit me with sticks! I'll go.

OurGirl picks up a rock. Oh, oh, please, don't throw rocks at me! I'll go.

But OurGirl puts the rock in her pocket and searches the ground for more.

OurBoy taps the stick on the metal railing, and it makes funny sounds. Tappity, tappity, tap, tap!

Then OurBoy throws the stick, but not at me. It goes high into the air and lands somewhere under some tall trees. He points at me, then to where the stick went.

"Fetch," he says.

What? I do not understand. I wish Chris were here to tell me what to do. Am I suppose to follow the stick and get lost under the tall trees?

He calls me to follow him as he runs to get the stick. I go and help him find it. Then he throws it again, points, and says, "Fetch."

Does he want me to find his stick again? Together we go and look for it. I find it! Here it is! He throws it again and again. Each time I run and find it, then bring it back to him. He loves this stick. I am glad I am good at chasing it. It is like a game. Maybe it is a game. A RunningChasing Game!

"Time to go home," OurGirl says to OurBoy.

Oh. I droop. OurBoy taps the railing with the stick one more time. OurGirl tosses a rock over the cliff, and we listen as it tumbles down a long, long way. Then they beckon for me to follow them back down the trail. Am I being invited back?

"Mina," they say as they pet me again and again. "You're so much fun. What a special Dog you are."

Me? A special Dog? But what about Chris? She is First in TheOrder of Things. But Chris could not go on this Long Walk up a mountain. And neither could Layla. That leaves only me. I can walk up a mountain!

Oh, joy, joy! I prance and jump and dash from MyBoy to MyGirl and back again. I will be your special Dog! I like your new game called "fetch." Can we play again sometime?

We race down the mountain, and I am happy, happy, happy because I am still part of OurPack! I love this Long Walk. I love them. And they love me! I am special.

When we reach the bottom of the mountain, they put my leash back on me. I understand now that just because they take my leash off, it does not mean I am being lost.

We begin the Long Walk home. Sometimes MyBoy holds my leash, sometimes MyGirl. With my harness and leash on, everyone we meet knows I am part of a good Pack.

The Dogs of the Neighborhood bark, "Hey, we told you that if you got lost, you can't come into our yards."

"I am not lost. I am one of TheGirls—and I am a special Dog. We won't come into your yard. And stop barking at MyBoy and MyGirl!"

Chapter 11

His Majesty on the Fence

Tension hovered like a thunderstorm on the horizon. With the unpleasant possibility of a fight breaking out between TheGirls and That Cat, OurShe made sure they were always separated. If That Cat came in, TheGirls were sent out into the yard. When he meowed to go out, the Dogs were called in. Whenever OurShe, OurHe, and the children left for the day, they put TheGirls outside. Sometimes the cold winter weather prevented this, and TheGirls were shut in the garage until OurShe returned. In a few weeks, when spring arrived, leaving the Dogs in the yard would be no problem.

This plan to separate them worked, for the most part. Without That Cat around as a constant reminder, Chris abandoned her plans for another hunt. Layla, scratched and bruised in her first and second meetings with him, had no desire for a third. Only Mina continued to think about him. She sniffed him about the house as she checked the Lookouts and promised herself she would behave differently next time they met. She had figured out a way that, maybe, Dogs and cats could live together, but she wondered how she could meet him again without alerting the BossQueen—and if he would agree to her plan.

🐕 Chris's Tale

That Cat remains on a long prowl. I sniff him every now and again. But I do not bother to tell Layla or Mina. Layla nurses her cat wounds like they are fresh. Mina bounces around full of ideas, but none that get rid of cats.

I enjoy spending more time in the yard. With my thick coat, being in the cold is pleasant. But the other Girls, mostly Layla, complain. Outside, I have a good Lookout. From here I sniff cows, but I never see them, even when OurShe takes us for a Walk. I wish I could find them. I want to try to herd them like I did when I was younger. I will ask OurShe to walk past cows on our next Walk.

Layla's Tale

I tell OurBoy and OurGirl that it is freezing outside and that they should not leave OurHouse. I know because I went out early this morning to make Puddles. Brrrr. I got back to the kitchen as fast as I could. But my feet, my nose, and my tail are still cold. Tiny Dogs chill easily. That is why I warn OurBoy and OurGirl, who are almost as small as I am, to stay indoors.

But they plan to go out anyway. They cover themselves in coats and then gather their books and those sacks of food OurShe makes for them. She never makes one for Dogs. I sniff their food and invite them to stay here and share their snacks with me. But they do not.

They push me aside, open the door, and say, "Stay."

Of course I will stay. It is icy out there. I do not like the cold.

Mina's Tale

As their special Dog, I take OurBoy and OurGirl to the gate every morning. Together we run out the door, down the steps, and across OurYard.

They pat me at the gate. "Bye. See you after school, Mina."

I wag my stub tail.

"You too, Thomas," they say.

I follow their gaze to the top of the fence.

There is That Cat. We stare at one another as the gate clinks shut. We are alone. Maybe now I can talk to him about my plan.

His tail gives a twitch, so I wag my stub tail in return.

"Hello," I say.

"Good-bye," he says, poised to leap down the other side of the fence.

"Wait. I thought maybe we could talk. Why do you say good-bye when you wag your tail in greeting?"

Slowly he hunkers back down on the top railing, still flicking his tail. "I don't wag my tail in greeting, like a dog. I whip my tail in annoyance, like a Cat."

"Oh." I sit down and try to be less annoying.

The ground is cold, but I want to understand about their special pet and all cats, so I sit still and wait. When he stops moving his tail, I say, "Cat, how do you get up on that fence? I mean, where do you keep your wings?"

"Wings?"

"Yes, wings. And how do you get narrow so you can slip through small spaces where Dogs can't follow? And where do you keep your Dog-stabbing knives? But most of all, what is your place in TheOrder of Things?"

His eyes narrow.

"You see," I explain. "Chris, Layla, and I know our places. That is how we get along. I figure that maybe we could get along with you, if we know where you fit in."

He does not answer so, after a while, I ask, "Should I talk to your boss?"

"Boss?" He stands and arches his back.

"Yes, who is your boss?"

He ripples his body into a long stretch that extends all the way down to his toes. Watching him makes me want to stretch, too. I almost do, when suddenly I see them—the knives! They slide out of his paws and then back in again. How sneaky! We Dogs wear claws on the outside of our paws, where anyone can see them.

He settles himself in a patch of sunlight along the railing and squints down at me. "I have no boss. I am His Majesty, Supreme-Ruler-of-All-within-the-Realm-of-the-Universal-Neighborhood-from-Rooftop-to-Treetop-through-Alley-and-Crawl-space-from-Cellar -to-Culvert. I go where I please and do as I please."

"Impressive. But what is your Job?"

He does not answer.

"OurJob," I say helpfully, "is to guard OurPack, OurHouse, and all that is in it. That would include you, if you like. We bark all danger away, and we would not hunt you, if you were one of us, but you'd have to stop using your knives on us. We can be in one Pack, Dogs and cat."

He peers down over his shoulder at me. "Do you really think that bossy queen of yours would agree to that?"

"I think she has to."

"And that big hunting dog? Does she need another scratch on the nose to make her agree?"

"We must all agree. We are Dogs, and we are invited into the house with you. OurShe says we have to get along. Maybe all we need to do is to decide what your Job is. You don't have to catch mice, if you don't like. I don't either. Chris can do that."

"What are you going on about? I am a Cat, and I will not be assigned a job. I do as I please. Sit in the sun. Sleep. Eat. Prowl."

"What is prowl?"

"A long walk."

"Oh, I go on Long Walks, too! I go with OurBoy and OurGirl in my harness and leash so everyone knows I am part of a Pack. Is that how you do it?"

"Certainly not! That's a dog's way! I go alone, and at night."

"But what's the fun of being alone in the dark? On our Long Walks, we play games. You like games, right? You and I are good at pouncing games."

"So?" he says.

"It's something we have in common."

"Why do you care?"

"Because, maybe, if we find something we all have in common, we could get along. We live in the same house, so we ought to try."

"That will never happen between dogs and Cats, especially with that bossy queen of yours. And that hunter."

I sigh. "Maybe you are right. The BossQueen and Layla won't listen to the Last Dog any more than you do. Dogs and cats can't get along because we're too different. You don't do things like a Dog, or care about TheOrder of Things."

"Of course not." He rises and struts along the thin railing. "Don't try to make me part of your pack."

"But even if Chris and Layla cannot get along with you, I think you and I ought to be friends."

He pauses beside the large tree that grows over the fence. "Why?"

"Because we are both special pets."

"Special pets?"

"To OurBoy and OurGirl. We are special to them. We're the same in that way."

"I never thought of that." He might be smiling. It is hard to tell with cats.

"My name is Mina." I wait, but he does not offer his name in return. So I say as politely as possible,

"Your Majesty, I've enjoyed talking to you as one special pet to another. But don't tell Chris or Layla we've talked. They wouldn't understand."

"Why would I talk to a dog?" he says with a twitch of his tail. Which is funny, because he is talking to me, and I am a Dog, but I do not point this out.

Then he flies up into the tree. I do not see any wings, but I see that he uses his knives to go up the branches. My claws cannot do that. He leaps from the tree onto the neighbor's roof, and then I know! Cats do not have wings. They have springs!

But I still do not know where they keep them.

Chapter 12

Something in the Yard

"Chris!" OurShe called. "Time for your medicine."

"Snacks?" Layla sniffed the top of the counter.

OurShe pushed her out of the way. "I don't need you underfoot."

She sliced three chunks of cheese, wrapped pills in one and gave it to Chris. She offered the others to Layla and Mina. TheGirls gobbled them up, but OurShe paid attention only to Chris, making sure she swallowed her medicine.

"Good Dog, Chrissy," OurShe sighed and petted her.

"Is OurShe okay?" Mina asked Chris. "Something has been wrong with her ever since the last time you visited the vet."

"Pay no Attention," Chris said.

"But I do. You're always telling me to Pay Attention.

And I see that OurShe is upset every time you return from the vet."

"Well," said Chris, "it's good you noticed. It's about the medicine."

"I took medicine once," Layla said, "and I am fine."

"I know," said Chris. "Come on, Girls. It's time to go outside and make Puddles."

The fresh air outdoors made Mina frisky. New leaves poked out on the tree that grew over the fence. And Mina could hear birds singing all around the neighborhood. After she made Puddles, she dashed back into the kitchen where OurBoy and OurGirl sat finishing their breakfast.

"Want to play?" she asked, wagging her stub tail.

The children pushed away from the table and darted out the kitchen door to play fetch with Mina. She had gotten very good at this game, but now, instead of sticks, she chased a squeaky red ball. The children would toss the ball back and forth between them, and Mina would jump to catch it. Sometimes OurBoy tossed it high into the air, and Mina would try to snap it up before it hit the ground. At other times OurGirl would throw the ball far across the yard, and Mina would run fast to catch it. They played many different ways while the older Dogs rested in their corner of the yard—Chris in a patch of cool dirt and Layla in the warm spring sunlight.

Soon OurBoy and OurGirl sat under the tree, and Mina joined them. Her nose alerted her that Something was nearby. She went over to sniff it. It was the size of a mouse, but it was Something else.

"Chris? BossQueen? What do I do about this Something?"

Chris's Tale

Mina tells me there is a Something in the yard. But why does she bother me about it? She can take care of it. I am resting. Layla wants to sniff it, too, so she gets up and crosses the yard.

OurBoy and OurGirl are looking at the Something and holding Mina back from it, so they do not see Layla coming. She does not bark, just scoops up the Something in her jaws. She tosses and shakes it. OurBoy and OurGirl shout at her. OurShe rushes out of the house and yells, "Drop it, Layla! Drop it!"

Because I am the BossQueen, I get up to see if there is a problem. I sniff the Something and know that it will not come into OurYard, or near OurPack, again.

"Good Job," I tell Layla.

OurShe should say, "Good Job," but she does not.

Layla's Tale

I got it! I got a Something! I play with it. But the play goes out of it, just like the Something Chris had.

This Something is different. It does not sound like the other Something. It does not smell like the other Something. It does not taste like the other Something.

But I do a good Job, don't I?

Mina's Tale

Layla drops it when OurShe tells her to, but it is too late for the Something.

OurShe does not say, "Bad Dog," but I can tell she is upset. So are OurBoy and OurGirl, especially OurGirl. She has tears in her eyes. They carry the Something into the house. Into the house? Why carry that Something in but the mouse out?

I peer through the see-through door into the kitchen. I see OurShe put the Something gently in a box and close the lid. I hear OurGirl say, "It was just a baby. It couldn't even fly yet."

OurShe says, "It must have fallen out of its nest."

Then OurShe, OurBoy, and OurGirl take the box into the field and bury it. Layla wants to help them dig, but she is told to stay in the yard. I watch at the gate, and when they return from the field, I try to wag them back to happiness. But they go into the house and close the door. They do not want to play fetch anymore. I hurry over to Chris and Layla, who rest in the corner of the yard.

"What was that Something?" I ask Chris.

"It was a Something that did not belong in Our-Pack's yard."

"Was it a bird? They said something about flying."

"It didn't look like any that I have ever seen, but if OurShe says it was a bird, it must have been."

"Birds come in OurYard all the time, and we chase them out," Layla says.

"They fly out," I say. "Why didn't this one fly away?"

"I was too fast for it."

"No, you weren't, Layla. It was just lying on the ground."

"Too bad for it. Now the other birds and all the other Somethings know TheGirls are on TheJob. Right, Chris?"

"Right."

"But if it's OurJob, why were they sad when we killed it?"

Chris closes her eyes—nap time again. I will get no more answers from her. I hear Layla's deep rumbling snore as I turn and cross the yard. Under the tree I sniff where the baby bird was found.

If TheGirls are really supposed to get rid of birds, OurBoy, OurGirl, and OurShe would not be upset. No one was sad about the mouse. I do not think Chris Paid Attention to OurShe's signals. OurShe does not like that TheGirls hunted the baby bird, so I will not do it again.

I wish I understood the differences between the Somethings. I thought Chris would know, because she is the BossQueen. But I do not think she can explain it to me. To her, everything is simple and clear: Pack or not Pack, OurJob or not OurJob. If I were BossDog, would it be this easy for me? I would not want to have to decide that Something is not Pack unless I knew what OurShe expected me to do. If only there were someone who could tell me about mice and birds and ThePack.

Chapter 13

Cat Talk

"Time for a Dog wash!" the children called as they ran barefooted out into the yard. They wore their swimsuits and carried a bucket and soap. OurBoy uncoiled the garden hose and OurGirl whistled for Mina.

"You're a good girl," she said, "but you need a bath!"

Mina, eager to learn a new game, tried to sit still while she waited for their instructions. Layla shuffled over and sniffed the bucket OurBoy was filling with water.

"No, Layla. This isn't for you." He pushed her aside but Layla nosed in closer. Suddenly the hose popped out of the bucket, wildly spraying the two Dogs. Startled, Layla limp-skipped toward Chris in the shade, and Mina dodged away. OurBoy grabbed the hose and sent a fine spray toward Mina, but OurGirl was the one who got wet. She squealed and wrestled the hose from her brother. Mina tried to figure out this new game as the children got wetter and wetter.

"How's it going?" OurShe stepped into the yard.

"Great!"

She looked from one to the other. "Hmmm. Did you wash Mina or did Mina wash you?"

The children giggled and Mina wagged her stub tail. OurShe wrapped towels around OurBoy and OurGirl.

"Can we wash the others?" they asked. "They don't move around like Mina."

"Layla's harder to hold than Mina, and likes water even less. Chris becomes a soggy mess with that thick coat. But I bet she would appreciate a good grooming. Want to help?"

🐕 Chris's Tale

I hate this hot time of year. I am more uncomfortable than ever. OurGirl and OurShe brush out my thick undercoat. When they tug, I want to snap and growl. Heat does not bother Mina, who bounces around and says something about finding That Cat. He stays out of sight, but we know he is still around. He is too foolish to understand that he is uninvited in a house with Dogs.

"It's too hot to chase That Cat," I tell her.

But she says she wants to talk to him, not chase him.

"Dogs do not need to talk to cats."

She says she wants to talk to him about hunting.

"Why? I've taught you how to hunt. He cannot even catch mice."

OurShe and OurGirl have finished brushing my fur, and I want to take a nap, so I tell Mina, "Go hunt That Cat. Do a good Job. Just let me sleep."

🐕 Layla's Tale

I do not go near cats with knives. Who would have thought all cats have them? Mina tells us they keep them hidden. I know they are sharp. I have a scar on my nose to prove it. When OurShe took off my bandages, OurBoy and OurGirl admired the marks on my nose. They told me I am very brave. I *am* brave for a small Dog.

Cats are scary things. I do not know why Mina wants to find That Cat. He might stab her. All cats can. Do not go near them.

Ever.

I learned this.

Mina's Tale

I want to ask That Cat about mice and birds, but many days and nights pass before I find him. He slips into the kitchen after a Long Walk, or, as he would say, a prowl. He springs to the top of the counter, and I hear him crunching his kibble. OurShe keeps his food out and his bowl full all the time. Layla wishes OurShe would do that for her, but Layla would eat it up so fast it would have to be refilled over and over and over again.

I wait for That Cat to finish before I address him.

"Good to see you, Thomas."

He stops licking his paw and looks at me.

"Thomas. That is your name, isn't it? I heard Our-Boy and OurGirl calling for you."

"And did I come? No. I am not ruled by a name, particularly any name they might make up for me. Why would I be? I am not a dog. I do not 'come'—or 'fetch' or 'stay.'"

"I know. I have learned that about cats. You are very different from Dogs."

"However," he says and pauses before he leaps from the counter, "when I hear the sound of a can opening and smell that moist meat, I run to the kitchen no matter where I am hiding."

"You can smell and hear that well? But your ears and nose are so small."

He drops down right in front of me. "Trash cans and tidbits, Mina! I can hear and smell just fine. How else do you think I track mice and birds and other things?"

"Oh! That's what I want to talk to you about! Do you actually catch mice and birds?"

"And other things." He crosses the floor and jumps onto a chair.

"Really? Like what?"

"Little moles, fat lizards, big bugs skittering all over the kitchen at night, lazy butterflies, jumping grasshoppers, and I especially love the flying bugs that buzz against the window." His eyes glitter. "I sit on the ledge and wait ever so patiently. When they move down the glass, I catch them in the corners. Must be quick. Some have a sting."

"Oh. That does not sound good."

"It's the best." The tip of his tail flicks, and his eyes grow large. "The challenge is what makes it fun. Ever try to catch a snake? Such unusual creatures, just one long curling tail with a mouth, and some have a dangerous bite. Hunting them takes wits. But they are not the most difficult thing I've caught."

"What is?"

His knives slide out and in, and his fur quivers. "Once, I caught a squirrel."

"I'm impressed." TheGirls have never been able to get one. But with those knives, That Cat could follow a squirrel right up a tree!

"I was so proud of that catch," he says, "that I kept its tail. I brought it inside, but it disappeared shortly afterward. I think someone else claimed it for their own. I don't blame them, really. It was quite a prize." He pauses and smoothes his whiskers. "But a squirrel is nothing compared to what I once heard. I heard about a Cat, not in this neighborhood, who caught—get this— a rabbit! Not just a springtime baby bunny, mind you, but a full-grown buck rabbit. It had to be as big as the Cat itself. That's something! What cunning. What speed and power that must have taken. I wish I'd been there to witness that—yes, indeed. What a Cat! I've never heard of a dog hunting something its own size, have you?" He stretches and settles back down on the cushion.

I cannot think of anything I would want to hunt, much less something my own size.

"That second dog of yours would have to hunt a cow!"

"Only Chris likes cows."

"Ha! If she plans to bring down one of those, she does have a high opinion of herself."

"No. She doesn't want to hunt them. She wants to herd them."

"What's the difference? I will tell you: A herder doesn't finish the hunt, that's what. Guess she's getting old."

Out the window the moon slides from under a cloud and lights up the yard. I put my paws on the ledge and see what my ears and nose have already told me—everything is safe. Looking into the yard where the bird was found reminds me of what I want to ask That Cat.

"You say you have caught many things. But how do you know which ones to kill?"

"I don't always hunt to kill. I'm not always hungry when I catch something. So I hunt it for practice, play with it, then I let it go."

"But how do you know the difference between those OurShe wants you to get rid of and those she does not?"

"How do you know the difference?" He squints his large eyes at me.

"I take my signal from her. I Pay Attention to her reaction."

"Well, there you go. She decides. Because I am His Majesty, I take care of those in my home territory by bringing them the leftover portion of my hunt. They decide whether to eat it or not. It is not my concern. Occasionally I've brought them whole live creatures."

I tilt my head and furrow my brow.

"To teach the young ones how to hunt, of course."

"How did it go?" I ask.

"Badly. Even when I brought them little things, it was too much for their abilities. They had no interest in catching food. Curious. I would have thought that after eating only what comes out of bags and cans they would enjoy something fresh. But they yelled and jumped about and tossed the creatures out the door. You see, they don't even have the sense to be silent and still so they can sneak up and finish the hunt. A pity. After a while I quit. With their size they could hunt anything. If they only had the desire—and the claws, teeth, and cunning of a Cat—they could catch many things. I suppose that is the problem. They are not real Cats, you know."

"Hold on." I twist my ear toward the street to listen to an out-of-place noise. Alert. A car slows down outside OurHouse. No one should be visiting us at night. I trot over to the window Lookout. The car slowly continues down the street. I watch until it is gone and listen until I can no longer hear it. Good. It is away from OurHouse. There is no need to awaken the BossQueen and Little BigBark.

"All's well, Mina?" That Cat asks with a wink.

"Yes. And no need to tease me about my Job," I say. "I am good at it."

"Ooo, touchy." He bats at me with a paw. I jump back a little before I realize the pat did not hurt. His paw is soft, softer than a Dog's. He did not use his knives. He stretches out full length on his back.

"The real difference between us is that you're a dog who worries about your job, and I am a magnificent Cat who brings gifts," he purrs. "How my offerings are accepted is not my concern. And I do confess I do not bring in everything I catch. I keep a great deal for myself. Most things, like birds, I eat alone. There's not much to share." He licks the long fur on his chest and then continues. "If you must find a rule—and understand, I am not one to find rules—but if I were, I'd say the rule would be—kill nothing for them. They toss away offerings uneaten, so don't bother."

"Except mice."

"Except mice. They seem to appreciate a dead mouse, but still they don't eat it."

"The BossQueen is never going to believe this."

"What? That I hunt, or that you talk to Cats?"

"Both."

"But you are not really going to tell her, are you?"

"I should, but Chris would only think I am foolish."

"But you are not. I know. Because you are not the only one who pays attention around here. This is another thing I've noticed—that bossy queen of yours is not as sharp as she used to be."

"What do you mean?"

"She's slowing down."

"She's just a little old, that's all."

"All I am saying is that soon you may have to decide many things for yourself."

"Chris is fine." But then I remember the chunks of cheese with medicine inside them. OurShe is sad every time she gives one to Chris.

The cat licks his paw and then curls up on the cushion. "Sure. Everyone is fine. All is well."

Maybe it is not OurShe I should watch but Chris. Have I missed signals from the BossQueen?

I lie down in a tight circle under the chair. I fall asleep as I think about what That Cat said.

The day begins when OurHe, who wakes up the earliest, enters the kitchen. I greet him with morning wags.

"Hello? Look at that," OurHe says, and reaches past me to pet That Cat. "You two friends now?"

That Cat zips out one door, and I out the other.

Chapter 14

Losing Layla

OurBoy and OurGirl hurried out the gate to play with the other children in the neighborhood. They did not take TheGirls. Chris, content to sleep in her patch of cool dirt, Paid no Attention. Mina, who was OnAlert, checked all the Lookouts. Layla, who sniffed for another Something, discovered the gate had not clinked shut.

"Chris, I think there is another Something outside the gate. In the field. I am going there to check."

Chris was sound asleep, so could not give her consent, and Layla was too intent on sniffing to realize it. She pushed through the gate and wandered out into the neighborhood alone.

🐾 Chris's Tale

Mina wakes me up. I am tired. I tell her to go away. But she says she is worried because Layla is gone. Gone? Where? Mina tells me that she went to check the Lookouts, and when she returned, Layla was missing. She goes on and on about how she thought Layla was away making Puddles, or inside looking for a snack. But when she found the gate open wide enough for a big Dog to go through, she sniffed that Layla had gone out. She asks me why I told our Little BigBark to do that. Was there danger out there for her to bark away?

"Oh hush, Mina! Enough. Why would I tell Layla, of all Dogs, to leave OurYard? Settle down and take a breath. Let's figure out what to do."

Mina suggests we sniff our way out of the yard and greet the Dogs of the Neighborhood. I do not understand why we should do this, but Mina seems sure we must. Fine. I get up, and we go out the gate.

What a strange and different place it is outside OurYard. Mina does not seem to mind. Maybe she is too busy sniffing to notice. I am not used to being out here without my harness and my leash. I feel odd. I give a shake from nose to tail to settle myself.

I see Mina dart back and forth, sniffing, as she moves farther and farther away from OurHouse. We go to places in the neighborhood I do not recognize. Have TheGirls been here before? Mina says I should remember this from short Walks. But I do not. She takes Long Walks, so I think she is confused.

I sniff, but I do not sniff Layla. Ah, but I do sniff cows! We pass by a field, and there they are. Cows! Finally, I get to herd cows. They have been waiting, all this time, for me to gather, sort, and chase them. I duck under the fence, and I am young again. But this time OurShe is not here to call me back. I can focus on TheJob of herding. I do not have to be both Lead and Heel Dog. Mina is with me. Come on, Mina!

I rush toward the cows. I know what to do.

"Move, cows!" I say.

Nip! Bark! Nip. They move. Nip! Bark! Nip. They move again. This way and that. They obey me completely and go where I command. My, but this is wonderful! I am Lead Dog, and I work the cows.

Mina keeps interrupting to tell me we must do OurJob, but I have no breath to explain to her that I am.

As Lead Dog I track the herd and know where they are heading. I have to direct them and the rest of my herding Pack, which is Mina. She is not a very good Heel Dog, perhaps because she is not a Shepherd.

"Pay Attention, Mina." Nip! Bark! Nip. "See? Follow my lead, and you will learn."

 ## Layla's Tale

So many good smells. I sniff around the fence. I sniff in the field. Oooo, but out here behind the house the smells are really good. There must be treats in these trash cans. So many trash cans! I sniff my way from one to another. But how can I get to the treats? I am a small Dog.

Chris and Mina! Come help me get these treats.

Hey, where are you?

I look around. This is not OurYard. Not Our-House. I sniff and sniff but I do not sniff OurPack. Where did they go? Where am I?

I sniff rain. I hate to get wet. I want to be home now, but where is it?

Mina's Tale

Oh, oh, I have never been so worried. The Boss-Queen forgot OurJob, Layla is lost, rain is coming, and cows are lumbering around in all directions. This is bad. I skirt along the edge of the herd but not too near, or too quickly, because I do not want it to scatter. I only want to keep up with Chris. I call to her over and over again, "We must find Layla, remember?" but she does not listen to me.

At last she slows down and lets the cows thunder away to the far corner of the field. They give Chris backward glances, expecting her to pursue them. But her sides heave, and her tongue hangs out.

"Are you okay?" I ask.

"Cows." She stares at them in the distance, but she is too worn out to take another step.

"We should not be in this field."

"A herding Dog's Job is cows." It is hard for her to turn away from them. "I am the Lead Dog."

"Yes," I say, "but not here. We need to go back to OurYard, OurHouse, and OurPack. They are OurJob."

She blinks and looks around her like she is uncertain in which direction she should go. Maybe she does not know the way home from here, so I start toward OurHouse. She follows. Her tail drags on the ground.

When we reach the gate, I say, "Chris, why don't you go in, and I will keep looking for Layla."

She flops in her dirt patch. I am about to ask her for instructions, but she is already asleep. I hope the BossQueen is better when she wakes up.

I sniff for Layla and smell the rain coming. A little shiver runs down my spine. I remember how bad it is to be lost in a rainstorm. Storms still make me want to creep inside and huddle into a tight ball. But Layla is lost, and I must find her. I zip out the gate.

"Hey, you!" I bark to the Dogs of the Neighborhood.

"We are here."

"TheGirls need your help."

"Yeah?"

"Yeah!"

"You can't come into my yard!"

"Fine."

"Fine. What's the trouble? Is something wrong with the BossQueen? Where's Little BigBark?"

"Little BigBark is lost. And I need your help. Can you sniff her for me? Is she in the neighborhood?"

The Dogs bark my question from one to the next until a Dog far away sniffs her and sends back the news.

"She is a short run from here. Are you good at running?"

"Yes, I am."

"She is near the Busy Place."

"I know where that is. On Long Walks we usually go to the mountain, but sometimes we go to the store and have to pass that Busy Place."

"Dogs get hurt by cars at Busy Places if they are not in their harness and leash."

"Oh, oh. She doesn't know about these things."

"If she's good at RunningChasing Games, she'll be quick enough to dodge away."

"With her slow old legs, she can't dodge away, even if she knew she should."

"You better hurry then!" the Dogs bark. "Hurry, hurry!"

But they do not have to tell me this. I turn and dash away as fast as I can.

Thunder booms so loudly overhead it hurts my ears. Fat raindrops splatter on the ground before me. I run faster than I have ever run before.

As I approach the Busy Place I listen, sniff, and bark for Layla. "Where are you?"

"Mina?" I hear her call back.

"Wait where you are, Layla. I'm coming to get you."

A car zooms by and blocks my view. The rain comes down harder. I am really wet now, but I do not bother to shake off. Through the rain, I finally see Layla across the Busy Place. How did she get there?

She limp-skips towards me. "I lost OurHouse, Mina. Do you know where it is?"

"Wait!" I bark.

She slows to a walk. "But I want to go to OurHouse. Can you find it?"

"I know how to find it, but you must wait for me." I want to cross to her quickly, but I know I must listen for cars.

Layla takes another step forward. "Where is Our-She? And OurPack?"

I am about to answer, but then I hear a rumble in

the distance. Not thunder but a car. Layla shuffles farther into the Busy Place.

"Pay Attention to me, Layla," I say. "Either you have to go back, or you've got to hurry across now."

"Hurry? But you said to wait." She stops, her brow scrunched in a frown. "Mina, I do not want to wait. I want to go home. I do not like this rain, and I am hungry."

The rumble gets louder as a car appears at the curve a short distance away. It is getting closer and moving toward Layla fast. I dart into the street and stand in front of her and bark with all my might to tell the car to stop, to tell it that Layla is in the way, that she cannot move quickly, that she was lost but I have found her, and please, please, please stop because she is part of MyPack. I bark and bark. Rain soaks my fur and pours down into my eyes, my ears, my nose, and my mouth. And still I bark. I stand in front of Layla, because I do not want her to be hurt.

The car skids with a squeal that makes my ears hurt. Then it barks at us! A bark bigger than Layla's BigBark! But it does not hurt us. Layla is so startled she yips and limp-skips to the other side, toward home. I back away from the car and bark as I go. The car moves forward again just as another car comes from the other direction. Layla and I are safely out of the way, but it passes so closely that our ears flap and water sprays up and soaks us some more. I hurry Layla away from the Busy Place before we shake off the water.

"It barked at us," Layla says, "but you barked it away. Did you see how fast it left us? Faster than any cat or Dog I have ever barked away. Wow, Mina. You must be a big Dog!"

"Come on, Layla. Let's get out of here. More cars will come."

"They will?"

"They always do. And they could hurt us."

"I am ready to be out of the rain, Mina. Where is OurHouse?"

"Follow me."

The Second Dog falls in behind me. Rain continues to splash around us. I hurry but make sure Layla keeps up. She limp-skips as fast as she can because she is so glad to go home.

The gate is still open when we reach OurYard. I let Layla climb up the steps to the kitchen door first, so she can bark until OurShe lets us in.

"Where have you been?" OurShe says. "We searched everywhere for you. Oh, Layla, you poor old gal. And Mina, look at you. Have you been playing in the rain?"

We enter the house and drip water all over the floor. We are about to dry ourselves when OurShe shouts, "Wait! Don't shake in the kitchen!"

OurBoy and OurGirl hold us until OurShe returns with towels.

Chris sniffs us and asks, "Why didn't you come in when OurShe called? It is raining outside, you know."

"I know. I went to get Layla."

"Mina, you are not supposed to leave the yard without a leash and harness."

"But Layla was lost."

"Lost? How could Layla get lost?" she mutters.

Chapter 15

Another Something, Another Hunt

OurBoy and OurGirl had saved their money to buy a new pet at the pet store. They had enough for bedding, food pellets, a dish, and a water bottle. They had already purchased a cage with tubes and a wheel for only a few dollars at a garage sale. The clear plastic exercise ball was included for free.

Today they would have a Something to put in it. Before they left for the store, OurBoy and OurGirl petted TheGirls in order—first Chris, at her Lookout, then Layla, in the middle of the kitchen floor, and last Mina, who pranced out to the car to see them off.

"Bye," they waved to her. "When we get back, you'll meet our new pet!"

Mina watched until the car was out of sight. "A new pet?" She trotted to Chris. "Will it be a Dog or a cat? Where will they get one?"

"I'm too tired for all your questions. Just be OnAlert when they come home. I will decide if the pet can join OurPack."

🐕 Chris's Tale

They bring it into OurHouse, and I bark to get rid of it. Their new pet is a mouseSomething. Imagine that! It is in a cage, so it will not run around OurHouse and be a danger to us. TheGirls would hunt it, but we are not allowed to go near it.

I did not want another Dog in OurPack, or another cat in OurHouse. I am too old to train another pup or to chase away cats. But a mouseSomething is no pet. It cannot be a part of OurPack. I tell TheGirls to wait until it leaves its cage. Then we can get rid of it. But Layla tries to get it now. OurBoy picks up the cage, takes it into his bedroom, and closes the door. OurShe sends us out into the yard, even though I tell her we cannot do OurJob from there.

I am hot from all that work and go to my dirt patch to cool off and rest, but Mina hovers and asks all kinds of questions about the mouseSomething. I wish she would settle down. Alert me when the new pet is out of its cage. Then we can hunt it. But for now, let me sleep.

🐕 Layla's Tale

Another Something! I want to play with it. Can I? Please?

I poke my nose into the cage, but I am not quite little enough to get in through the wire. I try my best, but it is so hard to do while OurBoy and OurGirl push me away. OurShe tells TheGirls to go outside. Can't I stay and play with the new Something instead? But no, out we go.

Then I get my wish! Chris sleeps in her dirt patch, so I look for a small snack. I nose my way inside the kitchen when I discover that the door is not closed. I find nothing in my food dish, but I hear OurBoy and OurGirl laughing. They are not in his bedroom anymore. And neither is the Something. They have it out!

Well, not exactly. It is in a ball, like a Dog Toy, only bigger. I can see the Something trapped inside. It tries to run away, and it makes the ball roll around! What fun! Can I play?

I jump into the room. I pounce right on top of that ball. It spins away—fast! It bumps into the wall. OurBoy and OurGirl yell at me. They are glad to have me play. Next I try and grab the ball in my mouth to shake it until the Something falls out. But I cannot because the ball does not fit in my little mouth. I try again and again, but it keeps rolling away. I jump after it, but every time I do, OurBoy and OurGirl chase me, hold on to me, and try to grab the ball for themselves. That makes it harder to get.

Come on, let me have a turn. When I get it, I will give you a turn. I am not like Chris. I share my toys and food with you.

There! I almost got it, but off it goes again across the floor. Before I get there, they grab it, rush off to another room, and close the door.

Awww, please! Let me in. I want to play some more. I am sure I can shake the Something out of that ball, if you just let me. Please.

OurShe makes me go outside. I do not even get a snack.

Mina's Tale

We are supposed to get rid of mice because they hurt OurBoy and OurGirl, but that mouseSomething is allowed in OurHouse. I do not understand. OurShe signals to leave it alone, yet the BossQueen wants to kill the mouseSomething when it escapes from its cage.

But the real danger to their new pet is not Chris or Layla. Another hunter lives in OurHouse, and he does not obey signals or follow TheOrder of Things.

That Cat sneaks into OurBoy's bedroom when everyone is away. I discover him while checking the Lookouts.

"Cat, what are you doing?"

He springs to the top of the table. He creeps toward the cage, crouches beside it, and peers inside. I do not like the way his whiskers quiver while he watches the mouseSomething.

"Excuse me, but I don't think you are invited into this room."

"Go away, dog." One ear twists in my direction, but his attention is fixed on the caged mouseSomething. The tip of the cat's tail makes slow looping movements while the rest of him holds completely still. I cannot imagine how he does that. I discover another difference between Dogs and cats. My tail is too small to wave like that.

He taps the side of the cage with his paw ever so gently. I want to call Chris, but she would bark and startle That Cat, who would knock over the cage as he sprang away, dump the mouseSomething out into OurHouse, and give the BossQueen her chance to get rid of it. That would be bad. OurBoy and OurGirl would be upset, more upset than about the baby bird, I think.

So instead of alerting the BossQueen, I step into the room and say, "Cat, I don't think you should hunt that mouseSomething."

"Hunt? No need to hunt. It's just waiting for me. Mmmm, how can I get in?" He bats harder against the cage.

"Shouldn't you be out catching the things that are a danger to OurPack, like mice, snakes, and bugs with stings? This mouseSomething cannot harm anyone. And besides," I say, as I take a step closer, "it's another special pet."

"I don't believe you."

"Oh, yes. It is. Like you and I. They would be very sad if you ate that special pet."

"I don't care."

My hackles rise. We Dogs can make them go up, but sometimes they just do it on their own. I try not to growl as I say, "Cat, that is bad."

He knocks the cage, and it scoots toward the edge of the table.

"Hey, stop that."

He squints at me. "What are you going to do about it?" Suddenly his eyes widen and glitter. "Perhaps you could help. I'll push it over, you pounce on it, and I will eat it. Or share it. If you insist."

"All I have to do is alert Chris, and she will chase you. You don't want that, do you?"

"Go ahead. Maybe I can strike a deal with her instead."

"Oh, I don't think so. She doesn't talk to cats, remember? She hunts cats. She and Layla."

"They can't. They're too old and slow."

"Are you sure you want to find out?"

"I already have."

"Well, what about me? I am not slow—or old."

"You wouldn't."

"I have to. It's a Dog's Job to watch over everything in OurHouse and keep it safe. Sorry, Cat."

"I'll use my knives."

"I know. But Layla survived. I suppose I will, too."

"I have other tricks," he hisses.

"Yes, cats have springs, and other secrets. They can get narrow, run up trees, and do all kinds of things Dogs cannot."

That Cat straightens up. "Well, I'm glad at least one dog admits it."

"But," I say, "Dogs have one thing cats do not have. We have OurJob, and we know how to do it."

He stares at me a long while. "My, my, aren't we the bossy Mina today? And just when we had become friends."

"We still can be, as long as you remember I always do my Job."

"A pity. You sure you wouldn't like to taste this treat instead?"

"No."

"Well," he says as he stretches all the way into an arch, then relaxes, "as a courtesy to His Majesty, will you allow me a head start?"

"Fine." I take a step backward.

"Thomas!" OurShe appears in the doorway. "What are you doing in here? Scat! Shoo! Get away from that hamster."

That Cat zooms past me out the door. He is gone by the time Chris and Layla rush up with their get-the-cat bark.

"Good Dog, Mina," says OurShe, and pats me. She closes the door so cats and Dogs cannot get in.

"Did you get That Cat?" Chris asks.

"Did That Cat get you?" Layla cringes.

"Neither. But I did have a talk with him."

"Why?" asks Chris.

Layla's brow scrunches together.

I walk into the kitchen for some water. All that talk made me thirsty. Chris and Layla wait until I finish lapping.

"What did you say?" they both want to know.

"Don't worry about it. I took care of it."

"How?"

"I told him that hunting a pet was bad, and I would have to chase him if he tried."

The BossQueen humphs. "I would have just chased him. Or waited until he got rid of that mouseSomething and then chased him."

"I would have barked him and the pet away forever," Layla says.

"I didn't have any instructions, so I did what I thought I should do. That Cat left, even though I did not chase him or bark at him. Their special pet is safe. OurShe signaled it was good. All is well."

Chris yawns. Layla goes to sniff about the floor.

I sit down to scratch my ear and think about That Cat. I wonder where he is, and whether or not he will talk to me again. I think I would miss it if he did not.

Chapter 16

Losing Chris

The day started like an ordinary and usual day.

The summer sun warmed the yard. Birds showed their fully fledged babies where to find caterpillars and bugs. That Cat crept in from his nightly prowl and slipped into a hiding place to sleep the day away. The hamster turned his wheel around and around, playing a squeaky melody. The Dogs of the Neighborhood stretched, yawned, and stood guard.

Maybe there should be a sign on days when things change. Perhaps the sun should shine purple, or birds should tap at the window, or the cat should yowl at the foot of the bed. Then everyone would know— today, things will change. TheGirls would not get up and think it was just an ordinary, usual day, when it was not.

Though the sun did not shine purple, no bird tapped, and no cat yowled, today was the day when TheOrder of Things changed.

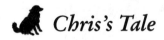 Chris's Tale

Layla's Tale

Chris? Are we going outside to make Puddles? Come on, please. I need to go badly. What am I supposed to do? BossQueen? Wake up.

OurShe says to go outside. I do. Even though Chris does not go with us. She opens her eyes but does not get up.

I lie in the sunshine and wait to be told when to bark. But Chris is not in the yard.

Mina's Tale

I am so worried. But it is not a dash-about-and-find-out-what-is-wrong kind of worry. It is a deep, heavy sit-and-watch kind of worry. Something is wrong, very wrong. It is the BossQueen. She does not go outside this morning with TheGirls. Then, oh, I hate to say this, she makes Puddles where she lies—on the floor. That is bad, but OurShe and OurHe do not scold her. They lift her onto an old soft blanket and let her rest there. OurShe puts a bowl of water near her. But the BossQueen does not drink. She does not eat. She does not even take snacks from OurBoy and OurGirl. So they pet her instead and whisper, "Good Dog, Chrissy, you okay?" If she likes it, she does not show it. She does not move, not even to wag her tail. I know. I Pay Attention.

Layla wants to know if it is okay to go outside. How do I know? I am not the boss. Layla asks me if it is time for breakfast. I am not hungry. I am too busy watching. I do not do my Job today because I must watch Chris.

Why doesn't she get up? I wait for her commands, but she says nothing.

Chapter 17

Lost

Layla lolled in her sunny spot outside, but Mina curled up across the kitchen from Chris. She did not venture near, but whenever Chris shifted or opened an eye, Mina's ears pricked up.

"Chris? This is not a usual, ordinary day so I don't know what to do. Give me some instructions."

Chris remained silent, but around suppertime, she lifted her head.

"Mina," she said, in a quiet but commanding whisper. "Why do you pester me? You know what to do. Haven't you been Paying Attention?"

Then she lay down and did not stir again.

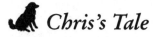 Chris's Tale

Today MyShe cries. It is because of me. I am a good Dog who has done my Job well. I helped MyShe move into this house and form this new Pack with OurHe and them. Now I am tired, and it is time to go.
I am a good Dog.
I sleep.

 Layla's Tale

Today my old friend died. I know because I sniff her. I sniff from her nose to her tail. I make sure. Then I tell Mina it is so. She will not sniff her, or come near. She just sits across the room and watches. I tell her not to worry. OurHe and OurShe know what to do.

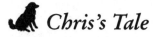 Mina's Tale

Chris said I know what to do, but I do not. How can TheGirls know what to do without the Boss-Queen? Who will I alert when Someone approaches the house? Who will tell Layla when to bark? Oh, oh, Chris. This is bad and I feel truly lost.

Chapter 18

The Dogs of the Neighborhood Howl

"Hey, you!" Every Dog of the Neighborhood knew something had changed.

"Hey, you!" two Girls barked back.

"We are here," they said.

"We are here, too," TheGirls said.

"You can't come into my yard!"

"You can't come into my yard!"

"Fine."

"Fine."

"Fine? But there are only two of you."

"Yeah."

"Yeah?"

"We lost the BossQueen."

"We can help. We will bark all around the neighborhood and find out where she is like we did when Little BigBark was lost."

"Thanks, but no. She is not that kind of lost."

"Oh. Is she dead?"

"Yes."

The Dogs of the Neighborhood were silent for a moment. Then it began—at first, soft like a puppy's whimper, but as more Dogs joined it deepened into a moan punctuated by yips. It rose louder and higher as it spread until all the Dogs of the Neighborhood cried out together in one long lonesome howl of sorrow for the lost Queen and her Pack. They poured their grief into the howl, into the neighborhood, into the sky. Not even the shouts of their owners could quiet the sorrowful Dogs. They yipped and barked and moaned and whined until gradually they grew empty, and the sound rippled away into the distance. The neighborhood fell silent.

Finally the Dogs asked, "Who is the new boss, the First in TheOrder of Things in your Pack?"

"We don't know. We're lost without a boss. This change is bigger than a move, stranger than living with a cat, and worse than being uninvited."

"Yes, we know. Things change. We are here."

Chapter 19

TheJob in Jeopardy

The day was a sad one for OurPack. OurShe wrapped Chris in a blanket and placed her special Dog in the children's red wagon. OurGirl wheeled Chris out to the field behind the house, where wildflowers grew and where OurHe and OurBoy had dug a large hole. They lifted Chris out of the wagon and placed her in the ground. They covered her with earth, and then they put armfuls of flowers on top. OurShe told funny stories about puppy Chrissy, heroic stories about good Dog Chris, and, finally, stories the children knew, about the old BossQueen. They said their thanks to her for watching over them, guarding them, and keeping everyone in their Pack safe. From now on all Dogs would be measured against their memories of her.

On her grave, they placed a large stone flecked with gray and white markings similar to those on her fur.

The BossQueen lies in a patch of cool dirt at a new Lookout, still on TheJob.

Layla's Tale

Is that a knock on our door? Did Someone come to OurHouse? Chris? Hey, Chris!

Wait, I remember. She is not here anymore.

No one wakes me up to do my Job. I am supposed to bark if Someone is at the door, right? No one tells me to, but I bark anyway.

Bark. I mean, BARK.

BARKBARKBARK.

"Hush now," says OurShe. "There's no one there."

So I stop barking.

It is hard to know what to do without Chris.

I lie down and wait for instructions.

Mina's Tale

I do not have any instructions. I do not know what to do. I watch the Lookouts, but when TheGirls need to be alerted, I have no BossQueen to tell. Without Chris, Layla does not know when to bark. How can we protect OurHouse, if Little BigBark does not bark danger away? When a Someone comes near OurHouse, she barks at them only after they are gone. When

Someone comes to the door, Layla does not remember to bark to alert OurShe. When I rush to the door, I bump into Layla, who is also heading that way.

"What's TheOrder of Things?" I ask her.

"I am the Second Dog," she says.

"I know, and I am the Last Dog. But which one of us is the Lead Dog?"

"I am the Second Dog," she repeats.

"I worry that, without a boss, TheGirls are not doing a good Job."

"It's the boss's Job to see that we are doing a good Job."

"I know, but who is the boss?"

"Yes. I am the Second Dog."

"Go to sleep, Layla," I sigh.

"I will be here if you need me to bark." She thuds down on the kitchen floor.

"I know," I say.

I just don't know who is boss.

Chapter 20

A New Lead Dog

Mina worried. She worried so much she could not sleep. No one noticed when she rose in the night, left the bedroom, checked all the Lookouts, and then curled up on the soft carpet in the living room.

She was so worried she did not sense when That Cat tiptoed into the room until his snub nose touched her pointed one.

"Oh, hi Cat. It's you. I haven't seen you around."

"I heard about the BossQueen."

"Yes."

"The news is all around the neighborhood." He rubbed against her side. "I cut my prowl short when I heard."

Mina let out a miserable little sigh. "Everything has changed. I feel lost all over again."

"I know."

"How could you? You don't understand about The-Order of Things, or the BossQueen, or about being Last Dog."

"Something like this happened to me. Once some-one close to me, in my pack, as you dogs would say, was hurt on a prowl—hurt by a car. I tried to help. I licked her and licked her, but she never woke up. I missed her so much—everything changed. I know how lost you feel." He purred softly and smoothed Mina with his face. "It happens to everyone at some time or another. Dog or Cat, it makes no difference."

"So," Mina said, "there is something we have in common after all."

That Cat's purr grew louder, but he did not answer. He continued to rub his soft fur against hers.

After a while Mina asked, "What did you do? What am I going to do? There is no BossQueen."

"Tonight, be sad, as sad as you need to be. Then tomorrow, well, tomorrow things may change again. You will be the new boss, I guess."

"Oh, no, that's not TheOrder of Things. We Dogs must decide among ourselves, as a Pack, who's boss among us. And Layla won't talk about it with me."

"So?" That Cat stopped rubbing Mina's face to step back and squint at her. "Listen to me. As His Majesty, who has seen the universe from top to bottom, I say, 'The one who should be boss is the one who can be boss.' You can. And Layla can't."

"But she's next in TheOrder of Things."

"No, Layla is second dog. She has always been second dog. You should take the lead. Not that it makes any difference to me."

"But I've never led any Dog."

"Excuse me?" That Cat looked hard at Mina. "I listen to the news of the neighborhood, and I know. You led Layla home when she was lost, didn't you?"

"But I can't boss anyone."

"No? Mmmm, I recall a day when you bossed a Cat out of a hunt. That's about as bossy as it gets. To do your job, you were willing to chase me, even when I threatened to use my claws on you."

"But Chris was so good at being boss. How can I be like that? She didn't leave me any instructions."

That Cat sat up sharply. "Fleas and furballs, Mina! What do you mean, she didn't leave you any instructions? Every day she showed you how to be a boss. You were paying attention, weren't you?"

Mina blinked. "Well, yes, I suppose I was."

"There you go." That Cat settled himself against her. "Besides," he purred before going to sleep, "it's a dog's job. How hard can it be?"

Mina's Tale

It is morning and just like That Cat said, something has changed.

"Hey, Cat, I don't feel so worried or so lost any-more."

But he is no longer curled up against me. Where did he go? Where did my worries go? Did he take them away with him in the night? Is it his Job to soothe and comfort? He is a very soft animal when he wants to be. Maybe That Cat has a Job after all.

I yawn and stretch as the morning sun brightens the room. I will always miss the BossQueen, but I have no time to worry and no time to fret about feeling lost. A Dog's Job is to protect ThePack and keep it safe—that has not changed. What has changed is that today MyPack needs me to be Lead Dog. I have Paid Attention, and I am First in TheOrder of Things.

I must check all the Lookouts. I must greet OurShe, OurHe, OurBoy, and OurGirl when they awake. Every time they return to the house I must begin the special greetings-to-you-we-are-happy-you-are-here bark. When they are gone, I must watch for Someones approaching OurHouse and warn them that TheGirls are on TheJob. I must tell the Second Dog when to bark all danger away and when to stop barking. I must play games and go on Long Walks with OurBoy and

OurGirl. I will Pay Attention to the signals from Our-She. I will pass on the instructions.

But I will not chase That Cat. Dogs and cats can live together. For all our differences, some things we have in common.

Layla's Tale

When we come in from making Puddles, OurShe gets the big bag of food out of the closet.

"Time for breakfast, Girls."

I limp-skip about the kitchen until OurShe puts our bowls on the floor. Food is good! When I finish I ask OurBoy and OurGirl if they want me to finish their breakfast, too. No? Okay. Then, will you pet me, please? Oh, thank you. I like that ever so much.

Mina goes to check the Lookouts. Can I stay and guard the warm kitchen? Mina says okay. She will tell me when it is time to bark.

We needed a new BossDog. And Mina is it.

This is good.

Epilogue

TheOrder of Things

Many, many Dog years have passed since Chris died. Old age took Layla, too, and left Mina as the Only Dog. She did a good Job, and her Pack remained safe. She was no longer an all-black Dog, for time had sprinkled her muzzle with white, but she continued to be OnAlert. Her eyes, ears, and nose were still as good as a Dog's should be.

One winter night her ears alerted her that a Something was in the house. She pushed open the bedroom door with her nose and crept out into the hallway. What was it? What had she heard—a rustle, a scratch, a whine?

Mina crept into the living room where the tree stood. She loved its smell, and so much excitement happened when it came inside, she wished it stayed all year long. That Cat wished so, too, as he often climbed up the trunk and batted at the shiny ornaments that hung from the branches. But OurPack brought the tree in only when snow fell and left thick white drifts in the yard for Mina to romp in with OurBoy and OurGirl. She was still good at RunningChasing Games, but she now understood Layla's complaints about the cold.

Mina looked around the darkened room. Many colorful gifts lay tucked under the branches of the tree, and Mina knew which ones were hers. A Dog Toy, hidden from her eyes but not her nose, was wrapped in a box, and a big chew bone, stuffed into a sock, dangled from the mantle. She knew how to wait for her gifts, but one gift would not wait.

"Oh, oh, I am so worried," cried a very small voice from a very large box hidden by the thick branches of the tree. Mina crawled under the tree carefully, so as not to knock off any of the shiny ornaments. She poked her head up and over the lip of the very big box and spied a very small puppy.

"Oh." He looked up at her. "Who are you? Are you my new mother?"

"No, I am not your mother. I am your Lead Dog. And you are my Heel Dog."

"I don't understand."

"You will. It is TheOrder of Things. I will explain it all to you. In the morning, you will meet OurPack. There's OurShe, OurHe, OurBoy, and OurGirl. There's also That Cat. He's not part of OurPack exactly, but he lives with us. We live here in OurHouse and go out into OurYard to play games and make Puddles. As Dogs, OurJob is to watch, guard, and keep OurHouse and everything in it safe."

Mina leaned into the box and, with her mouth, gently lifted out the pup. She set him down, but he immediately plopped over, stumbling on his big puppy paws.

He looked up at her with worried eyes. "Oh, oh, but there is so much to learn! How will I know what to do?"

"You will follow my lead. Come."

Mina led him out from behind the tree. The pup wobbled along at her heels. She lay down and curled up on the soft carpet.

"Now we will sleep so we can be OnAlert when OurPack wakes up in the morning. Lay next to me."

The pup toppled against her, and Mina licked his ears to comfort him, like Layla used to lick hers.

"BossDog?" he whimpered. "What if I fail? What if I cannot do this Job of Dog?"

Mina tucked the puppy inside the circle she made. "I will help you. OurPack is far too important for me to allow you to fail, so I will give you only as much of TheJob as you can do well. Tomorrow we will figure out what you are good at doing, and that will become your part of TheJob. We will add to that as we go along."

"But I don't even know how to be a good Dog."

"Don't worry. I will show you. All you have to do is Pay Attention."